UNDER ONE ROOF

Other books by Josephine Lawrence

Under One Roof

760753

Josephine Lawrence

Harcourt
Brace
Jovanovich

New York and London

Printed in the United States of America

Library of Congress Cataloging in Publication Data

Lawrence, Josephine.
Under one roof.

I. Title.
PZ3.L4364Un   [PS3523.A9354]   813'.5'2   75-12972
ISBN 0-15-192803-7

First edition

B C D E

Part One

Melinda Drew

1

"I," Miss Mary Hall said, "believe in action."

She had received me in the enormous living room of her apartment on the forty-third floor of one of Acton's modern luxury apartment buildings. Not for her the family mansion that, since her sister's death, had been converted into an art museum. Miss Mary, I had read in the news stories, was not tied to the past. Still, I thought, as I waited in the beautiful room with one wall entirely of glass, she was not a convert to contemporary art—her mahogany furniture in colonial design, the soft blue-and-peach coloring of the Persian rugs, and the low bookcases must rouse the envy of the period collector. The room was absolutely still; when Miss Mary came in, I was reflecting how long it had been since I sat in any room anywhere without hearing the sound, distant or at hand, of a tuned-in radio or television set. She crossed the half acre or so of rug before I could get to my feet, and, as she shook my hand, gently pressed me back into my chair.

"Don't get up—I'm so sorry to have kept you waiting." Her voice was clear and rather high. "Do you know, Mrs. Drew, you look exactly as I hoped you would? I'm a firm believer in first impressions."

She was a famous hostess, with a gift for putting everyone completely at ease, a gift that was rooted, I'm sure, in her very real interest in people. A superficial interest it might be—indeed, it could not be otherwise when the demands upon her money and time were considered—but, while it lasted, it was warmhearted and genuine.

We sat facing a sweep of late-afternoon sky, and I saw that she had no reason—even at seventy-one—to fear the light. Her naturally good complexion had been given meticulous care all of her life and was still lovely. She wore a gray tex-tured-silk dress and a pearl choker and stud earrings. All her dresses, she later told me, were cut on one basic pattern, only the skirt and sleeve length varying. For "interest" she de-pended, she remarked simply, on jewels.

Miss Mary waited while the maid put a small table at my elbow with a plate of heavenly-looking little cakes. She gave me my cup of tea, and, when we were alone again, leaned forward to say confidentially, "You're so exactly the right per-son. You have no idea how pleased I am."

My grandmother had always insisted that tea "loosened her tongue" and that more secrets were revealed at the tea table than at the bar—though how she knew anything about what went on in bars remained an unsolved puzzle to her bemused family. Anyway, after three sips of her excellent strong tea, Miss Mary began to talk fluently.

"I have a social conscience," she assured me. (As if I had

4

ever disputed it!) "A great many others know as well as I do what is wrong with our present society, but they do nothing about it. I intend to take action."

Her favorite word seemed to be "action," and that might be the key to her involvement with an imposing list of civic and charitable interests. It was a nephew of hers who had explained to me that, if I took the job of private secretary she offered, I would find myself an executive and a trouble shooter combined.

"Aunt Mary expects an awful lot," he said rather ruefully. "But then, her enthusiasm is contagious, too. She's never bored."

He had added that as of now she was "all wrapped up" in an effort to re-establish the Old-fashioned Family. Even if his tone had not capitalized the words, I would have been impressed. And curious.

She looked very much in earnest as she went on to tell me that she had decided one of the greatest causes of unrest and dissatisfaction among the masses to be the lack of decent housing.

"Oh, I know there's been a lot of talk about it," she said, brushing aside my attempted interruption. "But there again, it's nothing but talk. Or, if action is taken, it's futile. I may be the only person in the city of Acton to know the cause and be ready to apply the cure."

The honest explanation of the city's housing crisis, she said, with the superb confidence that characterized her, was the determination of young people to isolate themselves. They refused to live together and to learn from the past.

"People used to live together, in one house, under one roof," Miss Mary pointed out, her dark eyes earnest with feeling. "Two or three generations under one roof. Now what do we have? Every single blessed family has got to have its own apartment. It's getting to the point where I expect to hear any

5

day that every dog and family cat must be set up in his or her own apartment."

Before that happened, she was determined to "take steps." And she proceeded to outline these steps with a vigor and clarity that, I was to learn, were characteristic. One example, she instructed me, was worth a dozen theories. What we—she and I together—must do was to supply the power that would activate the practical.

I may have blinked a little at this pronouncement—the undertones were formidable—but as Miss Mary outlined her plan it was evident that to her, at least, it presented no difficulties. Briefly, what she intended to do was to buy one of the enormous old houses that were now a glut on the market. Repaired and furnished, this was to become the equivalent of the old homestead. All I had to do, she assured me brightly, was to fill it with a family. She made it sound as if families came in packages and might even be picked up cheaply if one watched the special sales. Of course I was being unjust to her; her interest in all so-called social problems was always genuine, no matter how unconventionally expressed.

The assembling of a "family" need present no real difficulties, she said with apparent confidence.

"You just advertise," she suggested.

She was prepared to advertise for two grandparents, a father and mother, one maiden aunt and one bachelor uncle, and not more than three children. Miss Mary and her sister had been brought up in what must have been magnificent loneliness in that handsome house now a museum. But she remembered the stories she had read, books in which large and happy families lived in comfortable confusion.

My job, she reiterated, would be to interview those who answered the discreetly worded advertisement. Other applications might come from friends of friends—one never knew.

"The one thing you must keep in mind," she warned me,

6

"is that to be accepted into the family, the applicant must give up the apartment or house in which he is living. The whole purpose of this experiment is to release space. Otherwise there would be no reason for these people to try living together."

I would not be expected to surrender my two rooms and bath, she hastily assured me; in fact, it would probably not be wise for me to be a member of the household. I must remain neutral, and, once established in the office she intended to provide for me, I would be in a position to deal fairly with requests and complaints.

"And no one is to know anything about anything," she concluded, so abruptly that I almost jumped.

This was more than I cared to agree to, and after a short argument it was decided that I might consult my lawyer, who is also my nephew. I gave Miss Mary his name and office address, and she must have called her own lawyer's firm before I got down to the foyer, because the doorman stopped me as I left the elevator to say there was a call for me on the house switchboard.

"I just wanted you to know that Mr. Simmonds says your nephew is a fine young man and an excellent lawyer," Miss Mary said without punctuation. "Good-bye."

Rick is not only an excellent lawyer; he is also a most comfortable person to talk to. A good listener is rare enough to be appreciated, especially by middle-aged, jittery aunts. What I wanted, I told him, after reporting the gist of my interview with Miss Mary, was to be assured that everything was perfectly legal.

"I couldn't afford to be sued," I said seriously, but he laughed.

He doubted there would ever be any grounds for suing, he said, and, although some of the aspects, as I had outlined them, might sound rather bizarre, the novelty of the plan had definite appeal.

7

"Fewer and fewer people are able to concentrate their minds on the possibilities beyond cut-and-dried routine." Rick, who will someday make an excellent judge, eyed me solemnly from across his desk. "I know you can hardly wait to plunge into this thing. Therefore why consult me?"

So the next day Miss Mary and I went hunting for a house. It was a revelation—to me, at least—to discover how many large houses there were on the market. As one real-estate agent told us, anything with more than six rooms was difficult to rent or sell, and the once-magnificent, stately dwellings, most of them unoccupied for decades, were the despair of owners, who often wound up selling their white elephants for taxes. Miss Mary's money had saved her family mansion, but hers was an exception. Many of the houses we looked at had been stripped of their elegant fittings, such as hand-painted china doorknobs, imported fireplace tiles, and silver (or silver-plated) faucets.

Miss Mary knew exactly the kind and size of house she wanted, and even the location. She stressed the point that it must be within the city limits, although she admitted that the family of her dreams had most likely lived in a small town or a village. For all her imagination, she had a wide practical streak, which, combined with her natural intuitiveness, kept her feet firmly on the ground.

"There'll be the question of transportation," she said to me one day, when we were having a drugstore-fountain lunch after an exhausting morning's search. "And schools for the children."

This was the first time I had thought seriously about the children, although naturally one would expect them to have a part in any family plan.

"But you can't advertise for children," I objected. "Every child has some kind of guardian, even if it's only the state. And

8

of course no parents are going to lend their own kids for this sort of experiment."

Miss Mary was sure it could be arranged. Perched on a high stool and eating a bacon-and-tomato sandwich with every evidence of enjoyment, she declared that once we had found the right house, and it was in order, the rest of her plan would fall into place automatically.

"I have a feeling that we'll find the exact house we want before we go home this afternoon," she said, and ordered a chocolate sundae for dessert.

Her optimism saw us through three more decayed and dreary mansions that afternoon, and I thought she might suggest that we skip the fourth address on the agent's list—after all, from what we had seen, a large house, if vacant, could be written off as hopeless.

Miss Mary, however, came from a long line of ancestors whose motto had been "No Surrender." She did weaken to the extent that we took a taxi to the northern boundary of Acton, and there, just within the city limits, we found a house that she immediately identified as the answer to our search. Once put in order, she assured me, it would be perfect.

All it needed, as far as I could see, was to be rebuilt. Four stories high, of red brick, it stood flush with the sidewalk, and it had eight windows (I counted them—they were all broken) on each side of the Dutch door. The interior was a shambles, but, oddly enough, the stained-glass fanlight on the second floor, from which a stairway descended on either side of the hall, was intact. There was a half acre, more or less, of "back yard" that evidently served the neighborhood as a trash-dumping center. There was only one bathroom, and all the fixtures, as we discovered in the kitchen, had been ripped out.

"The location is perfect." Miss Mary beamed at me. "And I'm sure the foundations are good."

That I conceded, since the house was still standing, but the thought of the amount of work and the outlay of money needed to make it habitable horrified me.

"Wouldn't it be cheaper to build a house?" I asked, but Miss Mary shook her head reprovingly.

"My dear, think of the time, to say nothing of the wrestle with architects and builders. I cannot endure the thought of it—'time is of the essence,' as the lawyers always say. I'll get the agent to push the sale through and start the repairs immediately. And you'd better begin your work. It takes more time and intelligence to deal with human beings and their lives than with tools and pots of paint."

My office, I learned in the next few days, was already rented, equipped, even to a young and attractive secretary, and waiting for me. Phyllis Porter was studying nights for her college degree, and she was an enthusiastic supporter of Miss Mary's theories. With the optimism of youth, Phyllis saw no reason why the assembling of an ideal family should present any real difficulties. She thought Miss Mary's terms generous—as they were—and predicted that, if we were not actually besieged by applicants, we would at least be turning them away.

"Look, for one year they're to have a good salary, no household expenses, and probably more comfortable living conditions than they've ever been able to afford." Phyllis patted her beautiful new electric typewriter lovingly. "In exchange for which they—they—"

"Exactly," I said grimly. "All they have to do is to move out of the house or apartment they're in, releasing it to those in search of shelter, and adjust themselves to living in a group. It's been tried before, you know—think of the various 'movements' that have failed completely."

When Phyllis retorted that it would be fun to see what happened, I made the mistake of challenging her to advise me where I should start.

"Well, there is an old couple in the apartment house across the street from mine," Phyllis said thoughtfully. "I see the old man dragging ash cans around—maybe he'd be interested."

She didn't know their names, or anything about them except that the old man was kind to cats—she had often seen him feeding stray cats bits of food that he picked out of the garbage cans before putting them out on the curb.

"He looks like a grandfather, too," Phyllis said earnestly. "With a white beard and spectacles that are always slipping down on his nose."

I thought she might be confusing grandfathers with Santa Claus, but the Santa Claus image had advantages and would appeal, I was sure, to Miss Mary. There was, however, the question of Grandma. Was Phyllis sure the old man had a wife?

"Look—" I sometimes wondered if Phyllis prefaced her recitations in class with this word—"the janitor work is always done by a couple. In my neighborhood, at least. Mostly they take on the job because they don't have to pay rent. Sometimes the wife does house cleaning and the like for tenants, but not always. It's just one way of getting along."

In my apartment building, new, modern, and clean, the superintendent had his own small staff, but that was just another way of getting along. Also he, the "super," could not have been much older than forty.

I was musing on the relentless penalties of old age when Phyllis murmured that perhaps I'd like her to speak to this couple, make an appointment for them to see me.

"I'm not exactly a stranger—I say 'good morning' plenty of times—and I could stop and speak to him, if you'd like me to."

I said that I would have to see the couple together, and so

we arranged that Phyllis was to ask them to come to the office, the next day if possible. When she explained that they would have to pay fares on two buses, we agreed that if they came in with her in the morning she could handle the bus tickets without embarrassing them.

2

At half past nine the next morning, Phyllis, who usually accomplishes whatever she sets out to do, ushered Mr. and Mrs. Caspar Lane into my office. Both old people looked a little apprehensive; later I heard from Phyllis that the taxi she had insisted upon taking had narrowly missed killing a cat.

"Nothing would do but we had to stop and make sure the poor creature was all right," Phyllis told me. "I gave the little girl who said she owned it—the cat was pregnant, of course—a dollar, and the cab driver swore under his breath all the rest of the way."

She introduced me to Mr. and Mrs. Caspar Lane and tactfully withdrew, promising to get us all coffee. I thought the Lanes looked as though they would like to go with her, but I hastily began questioning them, and the necessity for replying diverted their attention.

Mr. Lane was seventy-six, he told me, and his wife, Myrtle, seventy-three. They had lived for nearly four years in the basement apartment of three rooms, and in return for supplying janitor service had no rent to pay.

"That's the big expense—rent," Caspar Lane said seriously. "First of the month comes 'round fast if you're paying rent."

He was what used to be called a "well-preserved" seventy-six. But even in my youth the term had a suggestion of something pickled in brine that would shrivel if ever exposed to the air, and Caspar Lane did not have the appearance of one who feared to be exposed to the elements. Nor did his wife. Both studied me gravely, their blue eyes bright behind the same kind of steel-bowed spectacles I remembered my own grandparents wearing. Their clothing was neat, undistinguished, and dark, but something intangible, perhaps a careful primness, clearly indicated it to be their best and, as such, to be cherished.

Myrtle Lane sat very close to her husband, gloved hands clutching the black fabric purse on her lap. A small round hat shaped like a cruller rested on top of the flat coil of her white hair, and a dazzlingly white pleated frill of muslin or linen spilled out above the severe neckline of her coat.

Her husband's shirt repeated this effect of dazzling whiteness, and somewhere in his pockets I knew he must carry an enormous, dazzling white linen handkerchief—all grandfathers in my recollection did. Indeed, the Lanes so strongly evoked memories of my own grandparents that it was something like a shock to have them say they were childless.

"Which was one reason I didn't pay too much attention to what Miss Porter told us," Caspar Lane went on to say. "Something about grandparents, and of course it couldn't concern us. But Myrtle thought it couldn't do any harm just to drop in, as it were. Just like a woman, she was curious."

Myrtle beamed at me, and I beamed back at her. How far along would this world be if men couldn't excuse their own inquisitiveness by blaming it on a woman? Although I've often wondered what might have happened if Adam had kept his mouth shut.

"I think it would be nice to try something new," Myrtle said in a placid, cheerful voice.

So her husband asked, grudgingly, what was the idea, and I tried to tell them, hoping at the same time that I sounded realistic. Miss Mary Hall, I explained, was anxious to relieve the present housing shortage. Her basic plan would, if developed into a successful operation, release apartments, and perhaps houses, to be rented by those urgently in need of such shelter. To Caspar's objection that there must be thousands of people needing a place in which to live, I replied as patiently as possible that there was nothing to prevent Miss Mary from repeating her experiment, once it proved to be practical.

"I kind of hate to give up our apartment," Myrtle did admit, when I appealed directly to her for her decision. "You never know if you can find anything else. Besides, there's our things."

By "things" she meant their furniture and other household effects, although the few pieces of furniture were hardly worth storing (Miss Mary was offering to pay storage), and most of their other possessions, the accumulation of fifty years of life together, could easily be packed and moved with them. As it turned out, the two trunks they brought with them when they moved were left unopened in the attic of the big house, but I suppose it was the sense of possession that was important. They had something that belonged to them.

I took them to see the house on Wisteria Street that after-

15

noon, and Myrtle was completely enchanted—with the kitchen. It wasn't completed, although the amount of work already accomplished surprised me. I'm used to waiting three weeks to have a new washer put on a faucet, but Miss Mary was different. Her method of operation demanded an army of carpenters, painters, plasterers, plumbers, and they were all working at once, it seemed to me that afternoon. The Lanes were so fascinated I could hardly get them to move from one room to another, but it was the kitchen that captured Myrtle's attention completely. Evidently it represented a dream come true, and I rather felt that way about it myself. Caspar pointed out—he would!—that it was a large room and whoever did the cooking would have to take a lot of steps, but Myrtle reminded him that he complained constantly of the cramped space in their apartment kitchen.

"The two of us can hardly get in it at the same time," she said.

So she and I together happily examined the mammoth refrigerator, which, as she said, could almost arrange and serve a meal without supervision. The combined gas-and-electric stove, too, was the newest model, but what astonished us was that there was also a large and gleaming coal-burning range at the other end of the room. It was this that moved Caspar to admit approval. He had been following us about silently, and I thought I had detected suppressed enthusiasm at intervals, but it was the coal range that really won his heart.

"Now that makes sense," he told us severely. "You can't depend on gas and electricity, but a coal fire is something else again. Besides, nothing tastes better than toast made over a coal fire."

The lighting arrangements especially interested me. The entire room illumination was clear, yet soft, and there were special lights for the sink and cooking areas, places that in the majority of houses and apartments I had seen were apt to develop irritating shadows. Myrtle Lane went into raptures over the shelves and the pantry. Never in her life, she said, had she seen a kitchen with shelves so exactly *right*.

It was really amazing how much work had been accomplished in so short a time, and yet nothing had been sacrificed to speed. I didn't need the assurance of the foreman superintending the painters on the fourth floor to convince me of that. Nothing but the best material had been ordered, he said, and no time limits had been imposed. Instead, double the ordinary number of workmen had been engaged—which was, in his opinion, the only fair way to cover a lot of ground in jig time. Of course it required money, but what better way, the foreman pointed out reasonably, was there to spend it?

I thought that as long as we were touring the house the Lanes might as well have their choice of the bedrooms, providing they had decided to accept the role of grandparents. How much Phyllis had told them I couldn't be sure, but I doubted that the outline of Miss Mary's project was quite clear in their minds. Phyllis has the type of quick mind that darts ahead of her usual listeners, and she never senses at what point she has left them behind.

Since we were on the fourth floor, that seemed the logical point from which to start. Caspar rather fancied a corner bedroom, but I didn't really think he should have to climb three flights of stairs and Myrtle announced flatly that she had no intention of dying of a heart attack. A nice room on the second floor was her suggestion. Both of them were in earnest, and I began to wonder whether, after half a century of marriage, they would wind up occupying separate bedrooms, when Caspar suggested that the *third* floor offered advantages.

"There's only two flights of stairs to climb," he said persuasively, "and in one of the rooms at the back there's a little balcony where you can hang things out."

So Myrtle was what my great-aunt Seneth would have

called a "hanger-out." According to Aunt Seneth, there are women who simply cannot resist hanging things out, wet or dry, on any handy railing, balconies preferred. Evidently the desire was shared by Myrtle, for she brightened perceptibly.

"Which room on the third floor?" she demanded.

He took her hand and led her to the third floor, while I sat down on the lowest step of the stairs in the main hall to wait. I could hear Myrtle protesting that there were too many stairs, and I didn't have much faith in the bonus of the balcony railing to change her mind. She was still talking as they descended after what must have been an extremely brief survey, but it was Caspar who delivered their decision, leaning over the banisters as I stood up.

"The second-floor bedroom's going to be all right," he informed me in a satisfied tone. "Myrtle says I can smoke in it every night before I go to bed."

Myrtle's rheumatism must have been more painful than she ever had admitted, to induce her to make this concession, and I must say both the Lanes appeared relieved to have the issue settled. I induced them—not without some difficulty—to have an early dinner with me at a small but good neighborhood restaurant, where I had a chance to explain Miss Mary's plan fully to them. Naturally, they were rather skeptical at first, but then, as Caspar pointed out, no one should be too critical until the idea had been given a fair trial. It surprised me a little that both of them instantly approved the role of grandparents. They had always wanted children, Myrtle confided, and she, at least, had over the years visualized them growing up, marrying, and bringing their own children to see Grandpa and Grandma.

"Although it may be just as well," she concluded philosophically. "I don't know that I'd want them to see us living the way we do now—and certainly we'd never consent to be a burden on our children."

She was looking forward, she said, to meeting the other members of the "family," and she asked me to give her the list again. "It will kind of get Caspar used to them. I've always been a good mixer, but he is apt to be standoffish, just at first."

This Caspar denied. He was as interested in people as Myrtle was, he insisted, but while she expected everyone to make friends with her quickly he liked to be more cautious. Friendships had to ripen and season, his father had always said.

The "list" (Myrtle made it sound like the laundry list, I later complained to Phyllis) fascinated both old people. I urged them to say what they thought about the proposed members, but Myrtle, reading it aloud to Caspar, was too absorbed to answer.

By the time we had reached the dessert they were happily speculating on who was most likely to "inherit" (Myrtle's word) their three rooms. Caspar predicted an army of applicants, but Myrtle was even more sure that the third cousin of the landlord's wife would move in the day they moved out.

"She's always coming in to see the rooms," Myrtle told me. "Even though we've told her we had no plans for moving. The way she talks, sometimes you wouldn't think we were there."

Since Caspar and Myrtle had a lease, they were safe until the house being renovated was ready for occupants. I bound the Lanes to secrecy—it was Miss Mary's chief worry that the newspapers might hear of her project and reporters descend upon her in droves. That was one reason why we hesitated to advertise, however discreetly. As Phyllis said with unconcealed regret, we had enough material for a dozen prize Sunday features.

With the newspapers out, or to be considered only as the final resort, what other media offered practical help? I finally suggested employment agencies and real-estate agents, but the response was definitely less than enthusiastic. Neither Miss Mary nor Phyllis approved of this suggestion, and Miss Mary immediately perceived a serious flaw; her plan demanded the release of apartments and/or houses, she pointed out, and anyone consulting a real-estate agent would presumably be in search of living quarters.

"Remember, I'm interested in making more space available," she reminded me, "not in supplying tenants."

It was Phyllis who put me in touch some three weeks later with Elizabeth Hubbard.

"I got her," explained Phyllis inelegantly, "through Sharon Cameron at the employment agency. Years ago she worked in an office, and now that she's forty-nine and her children are old enough she wants a job again. I didn't tell her anything."

Phyllis managed to make this simple statement sound vaguely sinister, but I may only have imagined that Mrs. Hubbard seemed faintly apprehensive when she came into my office the next morning. She was one of those women who look completely undistinguished and at the same time completely competent. When she moved "nothing rustled or flapped," as my husband used to say, and when she was seated in the chair beside my desk her brown eyes were tranquil. Her figure, I suppose, might be described as matronly, and she was all in brown, small hat, coat, dress, gloves, and low-heeled pumps.

She did not know what kind of employment I was offering, she said, her voice matter-of-fact and clear, but the agency manager had stressed that experience was not one of the requirements.

"Since our two children were born, my only experience has been that of running a house and bringing them up," she said. "It is because they are almost ready for college that I am free again to do outside work. And of course we—my husband and I—will need more money for their tuition. We've had to give a good deal of financial help to various relatives."

The children were twins, she related in answer to my question. A boy and a girl, seventeen, almost eighteen.

No, her husband didn't object to her working, although he frankly preferred to have her at home. They lived in the house they had bought when they married; it was mortgaged, but not too heavily—at least, her husband didn't worry about it, although she did, she confided, adding that Miles was not the worrying type.

"I am inclined to be anxious, I think," she said, "and that is one reason I'd like to have a job of some kind. But the main reason is we need the money."

I drew a deep breath.

"The job of housewife and mother—" I began, and she laughed.

"I'm sorry, I *am* listening," she apologized, "but I know all about it. Providing the haven and so forth for a tired man to come home to, safeguarding the development of the young— believe me, I have learned the speech by heart. And is there any reason why I should not combine duties? Be a housewife, a mother, and a wage earner, too?"

This time I felt a little like the spider whose fly has walked into his parlor—that happened to be the first simile that came to mind. I'm afraid I beamed upon my innocent fly.

"You don't know how truly you have outlined the situation," I told Elizabeth Hubbard. "The success of Miss Mary Hall's plan depends to a large extent on the character of the woman who consents to assume the roles of wife and mother in what we're hoping will be the ideal family. It's a new idea, that is, an untried idea, and I'm sure once you get the full picture you'll find the entire project absorbingly interesting. Did Sharon Cameron tell you any details?"

Sharon, as I might have known, had mentioned Miss Mary's name and little else. I talked steadily for more than an hour to the apparently fascinated Mrs. Hubbard, and if her expressed enthusiasm seemed to be reserved for the very generous weekly salary to be paid her, it was also clear that she was impressed by the scope of the entire plan. Although I cautioned her that the approval of her husband could not be taken for granted and that his consent was necessary before any agreement could be signed, Mrs. Hubbard was mentally disposing of their house before she said good-bye. Miles, her husband, she assured me, would provide no obstacles, if no one asked or expected him to give up his work as head bookkeeper in one of the large city insurance companies. Evidently it was his wife who "managed things," and the arrangement suited both of them, I was sure.

"Harriet Carr will be simply delighted to rent our house furnished. I'll call her up tonight," Mrs. Hubbard told me on the telephone the next afternoon. "They've been living in a two-room flat—and they have three children! We won't need the furniture—you say Miss Hall is furnishing the house. Be sure and tell her we've released a two-room apartment, won't you? She may like to know her idea is spreading."

Phyllis immediately demanded the location of the apartment when she returned from lunch. She had a friend who was dying to find a place to live. But, alas, Mrs. Hubbard, queried, declared that the news of the possible vacancy, uncertain as the date might be, had already circulated through the apartment house and the "super" had a list of eight requests for the rooms when available.

"We're doing pretty well, aren't we?" Phyllis suggested, enjoying a respite from the phone. "There's Grandpa and Grandma Lane, there's Father and Mother Hubbard. Say, that's neat, isn't it?" She broke off to admire the coincidence. "Mother Hubbard—if we'd planned it, we couldn't have set it up any better."

I admitted that Mother Hubbard had a comfortable sound, and I was toying with the idea of providing a puppy—certainly if the family-life plan was to be complete, a dog or a cat might be included—when I remembered that I had intended to phone Miss Mary about the question of children. The maiden aunt and bachelor uncle of her specifications were still to be chosen, but it was the problem of children that made me uneasy. You could not hope to "borrow" three children for a year's experiment, no matter how impressively underwritten by the state's most famous citizen.

Miss Mary could not be reached until the next week—she liked to disappear at intervals, and only her lawyer and perhaps her secretary knew where she was—and in the interval I thought of and discarded a number of plans for including two or three young children in what was to be at its best only an experiment.

Meanwhile there remained an uncle and an aunt to recruit—the term was appropriate, I thought, and what Phyllis called "pep talks" might serve us as well as the government. Those irrepressibles Ronald and Jane Hubbard also offered advice—in fact, the twins were so enthralled by Miss Mary's plan that their exasperated mother was heard to complain that she must have wasted the best years of her life trying to give them a happy home background, since they were so eager to abandon it for a commune. In return she was admonished that, like most mothers, she was living in a rut and ought to be grateful for the opportunity to go forward. Parents, Jane told anyone who would listen, were automatically opposed to progress.

She stopped in at the office after school one afternoon (if they couldn't talk to anyone at school about Miss Mary's plan, they simply had to talk to me or burst, Jane said) and tactfully inquired how much longer I thought it would be before "everybody was lined up." She managed to convey the impression that time was being wasted. What, she asked politely, was the "hitch"?

"Well, if you must know, aside from the question of where

we are to find the children," I answered, "I'm working on the problem of a maiden aunt. And a bachelor uncle. What do you suggest?"

"You mean 'whom,' don't you?" Jane grinned at me, giving her red hair a toss. "But I see what you mean. I don't suppose you'd like me to ask some of the kids at school? I could pretend I was collecting material for an extra paper on human relations."

I thanked her, but reiterated that any kind of discussion at school would annoy Miss Mary. Whereupon Jane informed me that all adults were unreasonable and the pity of it was that they had most of the money.

"I'll bet I could have collected a family in less than a week," she said confidently. "Ronnie feels the same way. He's all for advertising, and he's even written some good display copy that's really super."

I doubted if the type of maiden aunt we wanted would be attracted by any kind of display advertising, but I had to admit that I had no definite ideas to work on. Jane shook back her red mane and gave me a pitying smile.

"I suppose you want someone who likes to live at the YWCA?" She stood up, tall and slim and assured. "Although," she added, rather vaguely, "I guess they are not as strict as in my mother's day."

After she left, I had half an hour, before Phyllis returned from lunch, in which to consider the possibilities offered by the YWCA. The main branch was located on the other side of the city, and I knew little about the fifty or so women who lived there, a few transient, most of them permanent, and all employed. The handsome modern building was a memorial to one of Acton's most successful businesswomen, who had not only bequeathed the money for its erection but had also left it heavily endowed. The rates for room and board were low in

24

consequence and had resulted in a perpetual, and long, waiting list.

That evening I telephoned the admissions secretary from home. I like as much as any other working woman to keep my evenings for myself, but Miss Mary's insistence on secrecy was more important.

Elinor Waters also liked her evenings free, I was sure, but she was a good-natured, friendly woman, who assured me that she had all the time in the world to listen and that someone was "always calling me up" about YWCA work.

Did she, I asked, know of any woman, preferably middle-aged, who would be interested in acting as maiden aunt to an old-fashioned household? Even to myself the question sounded idiotic, and I was prepared for Elinor Waters's answer.

"Is it a gag?" she demanded. Then, assured that I was in earnest, "You must be kidding," she insisted.

She chuckled all through my careful explanation and, when finally persuaded that I was not joking, said doubtfully that she supposed she could put up a notice on the bulletin board.

"Most of the girls here are under thirty," she added as an afterthought. "They might think it would be fun to give it a try."

My maiden aunt, I repeated firmly, must be over forty at least. She might even be in her fifties and still qualify. Where did single women in those age brackets live, I asked.

"And for heaven's sake, no bulletin-board notices," I added. "Publicity is the last thing we want, at least until the details are settled. And remember, one of the main objectives is to make more housing available. I don't think occupancy at the YW is one of Miss Mary's worries."

Elinor admitted that single women making "decent" salaries usually set up their own apartments. A large number of them, she thought, were "loners," and those who shared apartments placed thrift above privacy. She could give me a couple of names, if I insisted, but I was not to count on winning any arguments.

My regular schedule was pulled askew the next morning when I reached the office to learn that Phyllis was suffering what she croakingly described on the phone as a low cold and a high fever. She offered to send me a friend to act as her substitute, a young woman who, Phyllis said, had been the private secretary of a bank president before her marriage and retirement. But I thought I could manage (a decision that appeared to please Phyllis), and although I didn't mention it, I felt for some reason that her absence gave me more freedom in my pursuit of the maiden aunt. Before I had taken off my coat I had phoned one of the two numbers Elinor Waters had given me and had made an appointment for eleven-thirty that morning at the bookshop where Miss Violet Mudd was manager and chief clerk. She was also, I discovered, the only clerk. A short, stout woman, fiftyish, wearing slacks and a tailored shirt with a bow tie, she was eating a sandwich at a desk in the rear of the small, book-crammed shop.

"Sorry I couldn't come to your office," she apologized, extending her right hand while she brushed crumbs off her shirt front with the left. "But I'm the entire staff, up to five-thirty. Then my nephew takes over till ten P.M."

Her voice was clear and cultivated, and if ever I saw a contented woman she was one. Instinctively I realized that there was small hope of persuading her to alter her life style. Yet, since I was here and Elinor must have known something about her, I couldn't just leave without an explanation.

"Can I get you some hot tea?" she was saying, as she removed a pile of books from a chair so that I could sit down. "The drugstore will send it in. Or would you rather have coffee?"

I thanked her and said, truthfully, that I had a luncheon appointment for one o'clock. Was she, I inquired bluntly, at all interested in becoming a part of a modern social experiment, one that offered an unusual opportunity for studying human relations? (Personally, I was getting fed up with the human-relations bit, but I foresaw I would have to live with it for months to come.)

Miss Mudd's intelligent light-blue eyes studied me for a moment. Absently she ruffled her short-cut sandy hair faintly streaked with gray.

"Why should I be?" she asked pleasantly.

Purely as a new, untried experiment, I said. "One that may work, or may not. But you will not be bored—I'm sure of that."

Miss Mudd swallowed a sip of tea and fished a package of cigarettes from under the sea of papers on her desk. "Smoke?"

I declined, and she said that she had given up smoking a year ago. Two men came into the shop at that moment, and she eyed them alertly. "Browsers," she identified them, and returned her attention to me.

"I have yet to be bored," she said, beginning to fold the sandwich paper into a neat square. "But I might conceivably need an ace in the hole one of these days. Tell me what's on your mind."

A confused feeling that I was the one being interviewed assailed me. I would have to be definite. I needed, I said quickly, a maiden aunt, and at once.

"At least I must have her commitment," I went on. "She's necessary if the family is to be complete."

Violet Mudd looked at me with a spark of laughter in her blue eyes. "What is a maiden aunt?" she asked gravely.

In this instance the maiden aunt represented an ideal, I admitted, but, analyzed, she was not a complicated character. As

I set forth Miss Mary's plan in detail, I watched my listener's incredulity give way to interest, in turn to be replaced by admiration and, finally, cautious approval.

"It might work," she said thoughtfully, when I had finished. "Anyway it's worth a try. Not many wealthy women have that much imagination—I hope Miss Hall won't be disappointed."

However, in spite of her apparently genuine enthusiasm, I could not induce Violet Mudd to consider the role of maiden aunt. She couldn't endure the lack of privacy, she insisted; when she went home at night she was too tired to manufacture conversation. Her freedom was priceless to her, and nothing could induce her to surrender it.

3

It should not have surprised me, perhaps, but it did, this almost fanatical determination of the single woman to live
alone. Those who shared apartments were in the under-thirty
class, but even they seemed to have developed the same fierce
resolve to sever home ties. By the time I had interviewed half a
dozen assorted types I began to wonder if there would ever be
enough separate roofs to go around.

"The women from forty to fifty are practically militant," I
told Miss Mary, who was, I suspected, becoming a bit impatient. "They give the impression of retreating to their castles
and pulling up the drawbridge. In fact, they as much as admit
they have 'escaped' from family living, and why should they
return?"

Miss Mary said she thought I exaggerated, and she was sure I would capture—only that wasn't her term—an aunt, and an uncle, before the first of March, the date set for the "moving in." She had succeeded in "rounding up" (the Hubbard boy's inelegant phrase) three young children who would complete the circle. Robert, Leila, and Holly Price, ages seven, six, and five, respectively, were the grandchildren of one of Miss Mary's closest friends. Both parents were planning a yearlong European trip and were delighted, she said, to be able to leave their youngsters in safe hands.

It was Violet Mudd, bless her, who solved the problem of finding a maiden aunt for me. If I was still interested, she phoned to say one rainy morning, she thought that a Miss Victoria May might be suitable. They had both been enrolled in an evening course in fiction writing, Violet said.

"I dropped out, but as far as I know Miss May is staying with it. I looked her up in the phonebook, in case you want her number."

Victoria May, who came to the office late the next afternoon, was an earnest, introverted woman, who looked younger than her forty-seven years. Her features were dominated by the huge, square-shaped dark rims of her glasses, and, although perfectly neat, she gave the impression of not being very much interested in the clothes she wore—a grayish brown skirt and jacket and a black turtleneck pull-over. She had closely cropped grayish brown hair and wore no jewelry of any kind.

Yes, she had met Violet Mudd in one of the evening classes at the Community College that winter. And although Violet knew that she had a job as head of the typing pool in one of the city's large firms, she, Violet, had seemed to think that she could do better.

"I ought to tell you, I suppose, that I don't get a very large salary and that there is absolutely no hope of advancement,"

Victoria May said, trying to tuck her feet under her chair, a nervous mannerism I had associated with young girls applying for their first jobs.

Her working hours were more important to her than the salary, she declared, when I asked why she did not try for something better.

"We get off at four at the office and I can be home by five," she told me. "I don't bother much with dinner and I have my evenings for writing. I'm working on a novel."

Her time in the short-story class had not been wasted, she added seriously, evidently fearing criticism.

"The most valuable thing it taught me was that I'm not the short-story type of writer. The novel is more my forte. Only, of course, it is horribly expensive, in terms of both money and time—and there is never any guarantee that a whole year's work, or two or three years' work, won't be a complete loss."

She stirred restlessly and evidently considered the interview over. In fact, she looked startled when I suggested that perhaps we should discuss the topic I had in mind.

"Oh! I'm afraid I didn't pay very close attention to Violet Mudd," she apologized. "Something about a family group, isn't it? I don't think I would fit into a family. My youngest sister has four children and is always after me to come and live with her. Of course it would ruin my writing, to say nothing of my nerves."

Not for the first time, I found myself sympathizing deeply with the unattached woman. Why should she be considered an answer to the prayers of the woman with a husband, children, and a home whenever these blessings became—as they do at one time or another—intolerable burdens? Why should wives and mothers alternately pity and despise the spinster? More power to her if, as I suspected, she has begun to fight for and win her own salvation.

However, as of now I had no intention of cheering the

crusaders. My conscience barely twinged, for I reminded myself that Miss Mary's experiment was for a year only, not a lifetime. Besides, Victoria May's personal demonstration for freedom was too weak to have any value as a contribution to the cause. I suspected she ate skimpy meals and worried about the rent on her one-room apartment.

"Let me tell you about Miss Mary Hall's splendid idea," I began briskly. "You may, if you are willing to take part, have to give up your apartment—"

A half hour later I was still talking. The real stumbling block was Miss Mary's mandate that no woman in the household should "go to business" or hold any kind of outside job. The men, yes, they were free to continue their work, but the women must function as homebodies—Phyllis told me she considered that a disgusting label, one that reminded her of crawling insects. Victoria May admitted that her job could not be called important, that she found it boring and poorly paid, but that it *did* represent independence. Until her book was finished and published, she was quite prepared to live at what she called a substandard level.

It was at this point that I had an inspiration. Could she afford, I said solemnly, could any writer afford, to shut herself off from the endlessly complicated and fascinating study of actual people? What I was offering her, I declared, was a priceless opportunity to develop and enrich her art. No novelist could hope to write convincingly of life, I warned the astonished woman, who looked petrified by my eloquence (and no wonder!), unless first aware of its infinite variety.

"Hasn't someone said that every person's life contains enough material for a book? By spending a year with Miss Mary's 'family,' think of the knowledge of human nature you will have acquired."

I honestly do not believe it was my oratory that persuaded Victoria May to join the experiment. It was far more likely the salary she was offered and the vision it promised of release, for twelve months at least, from nagging worry about living expenses. I thought it would probably be difficult for her at first to adjust to spending her evenings with a group, instead of pounding happily away on her typewriter in delightful isolation. Something must be worked out, I told myself, to give her some free time for writing during the day. Even in the good old days, I reasoned, maiden aunts could not have been on call from morning till night.

It was rather disconcerting to have Miss Mary suggest that perhaps we should have *two* maiden aunts and *two* bachelor uncles. There I was, exhausted from the effort needed to produce one aunt, and to be asked to face the prospect of finding another was a little too much.

"Why do we need two?" I argued. "They might not get on well together. In fact, I'm sure they wouldn't. You are going to have three women in the house all day as it is, and heaven only knows what they'll do. Things could be sticky without adding a fourth female."

Miss Mary sighed, but yielded good-temperedly. The second maiden aunt, she said, could be added later if needed. It was just that she had wondered if Victoria May had any experience with children. Did I know?

I did not know and I had omitted to ask. All my effort and attention had been centered on selling the family idea to Victoria. Now that I had time to reflect, I was certain that she knew little if anything about children, and although I had explained about the Hubbard twins and the three small Price children, Victoria had made no comment.

"The whole idea gets crazier by the minute, doesn't it?" Phyllis, restored to blooming health and recharged with curiosity, said happily that afternoon. "How are you going to tackle the bachelor uncle bit?"

Men, she added, in a belated effort to be more optimistic,

loved comfort. She advised me to find one who couldn't cook—her boyfriend was a better cook than she was, but he always left the washing up to her, she said.

"A bachelor who can't cook and thinks woman's duty is to sew the buttons on his shirts might be interested in this sort of thing. And, say, I've a thought—while you are about it, couldn't you settle for one who's young, good-looking, and has a car? He could take me out when he gets tired of family life."

My job was to find a bachelor middle-aged or older, I reminded her severely. No, I had no matchmaking plans, I hastily inserted when she accused me of planning a romance. No, I didn't feel that I should have Victoria May's happiness at heart—she wasn't interested in marriage, and the confirmed bachelor I intended to find would certainly be indifferent to the wiles of any female.

If my search for the maiden aunt had been difficult, trying to track down the ideal bachelor uncle was ten times more so. For one thing, it was next to impossible to brief a man without revealing too much of Miss Mary's plan. Then, too, the masculine mind seemed geared to a compulsive search for flaws. The entire setup lacked common sense, I was informed again and again. What was lacking was the factual approach, I heard endlessly. Why waste time and money on a wild scheme doomed to failure from the start?

"You don't know it's a failure," I objected. "It hasn't been tried. Plenty of people have laughed at idealists and felt like apologizing later. You're not being asked to risk your life, only to take part in what is really a new—that is, new to this generation—concept of living. Haven't you any desire to forsake the cut and dried?"

The bachelors to a man declared themselves to be satisfied with the cut and dried. Like the spinsters (only they would perish before admitting it), they were intent on escape from possessive family ties. Few of them were really chatty, and they were all reluctant to go into details, but even the most cautious revealed a passionate distrust of home life as they remembered it. Their few utterances were so vivid that I could fairly visualize each one of them as he shook the hearth ashes from his feet forever.

Miss Mary, who had inherited an inexhaustible stock of sayings from an old nurse, assured me that it is always darkest just before the dawn. This I took to mean that the bachelor uncle would present himself before I was committed to a rest home. I did sleep like the proverbial log that night, but it was from sheer exhaustion, not renewed hope.

I was still asleep the next morning when Miss Mary telephoned. She had been up for an hour, she said proudly—late sleepers are always consumed with pride when they break their pattern. At first I thought the announcement that she had breakfasted at half past eight was her only reason for calling, but I was wrong. She had, she told me, her voice trembling with excitement, discovered our bachelor. Miss Mary has always been generous, and now she was presenting me with a share in a man I'd never seen.

"He's forty-seven." She was so excited she stuttered slightly. "And he's intelligent—that's one reason I think he'll be interested in taking part in my plan. Do let me know what you think of him, won't you?"

She actually hung up then and was greatly surprised, when I called her back, to learn that she had not told me the man's name or where I could reach him. He was, I learned, a patent lawyer with an office in downtown Acton. His name, Reade Coleman, meant nothing to me, although Miss Mary rather thought that he had been a friend of one of my cousins. He had given an informal talk to the members of her women's club the night before she phoned me, Miss Mary said.

"He was very good. He said that women are ingenious and often devise simple gadgets that are worth patenting. He wasn't a bit patronizing, either. And during the coffee hour afterward I heard that he's never been married. The wife of St. Margaret's rector is distantly related to him, I believe. I could speak to her, don't you think?"

I was still trying to sort this out when we said good-bye.

Miss Mary must have done more than speak to the rector's wife, because it was Reade Coleman himself who called me at the office two days later. He was perfectly willing to come in and listen to the details of my project—well, Miss Mary's project—if I understood at the outset that he couldn't be involved. He gave me the feeling that he was doing this to please Miss Mary, and I wanted to tell him that more than that was involved. Miss Mary was determined to prove a theory, and she quite clearly believed that once she had her chessmen arranged, so to speak, they could be depended upon to make the right moves automatically.

Reade Coleman was Phyllis's type—she assured me of this at intervals during the next two weeks. He was lean and tall, with what she described as a "craggy" face, dark-eyed, and with a thick crop of iron-gray hair. It was his voice that I would have mentioned first, but then, I am sensitive to voices. Reade Coleman's voice was pleasant, unhurried, and deep, but not remotely resembling a masculine growl.

"Frankly, I'm a cynic," he warned me, seating himself in the chair by my desk. "Miss Mary hasn't been too definite about this thing, but from what she's told me I gather it is an attempt to dissect human nature, however you describe it."

The plan, I explained patiently, would probably best be considered as a social experiment. "People have forgotten how to live together, is Miss Mary's contention. I think you'll admit she is right to a large extent. The housing situation—and that's really the main issue—wouldn't be nearly as serious as it is if people could be persuaded to live in—well, in groups."

"But groups would have to have some place to live." Reade

36

Coleman was also trying to be patient, although patience was evidently not his strong point. "I don't understand what you're trying to accomplish. Miss Mary was extremely vague."

It was Miss Mary's idea to accomplish two things, I said.

"One, to release apartments, and perhaps even a house or two, for tenants desperately in need of shelter. Not necessarily the poor, but middle-class people who need decent places in which to live. Two, Miss Mary remembers an era when adult members of a family remained at home instead of setting up their own separate quarters. Yes, even married couples—" I hastily forestalled his objection—"but not always, of course. It is Miss Mary's contention that this accent on family resulted in happier and more contented lives."

Reade Coleman shook his head.

"Don't you believe it," he almost barked. "Think of them all cooped up together, with probably one mastermind ruling the roost. There would be sure to be one dictator in every group, and the meek would be trampled on mercilessly, with no way to escape."

When I suggested that it might be different now—women especially, I reminded him, had had more experience in standing up for their rights—he laughed.

"I thought your idea was to have one big happy family," he said sardonically. "No, if the scheme has ever worked, it was because someone was ruler and the rest of the unfortunates consented to be slaves."

He added that he was surprised a woman of my intelligence—why does being complimented on her intelligence usually annoy a woman?—should have any faith in the success of a venture so clearly doomed to fail.

To this I retorted that only a fair trial could prove him right and as a lawyer he must admit he had no evidence on which to base his judgment. Neither had I, he was quick to point out.

"It won't work, it can't work," he kept repeating. "The only community-living plan that has survived this concept is that followed by monks and nuns. And even that is not a good comparison—the strain of normal family relationships is completely absent in the religious orders."

The strain of family relationships was not easing to any appreciable extent among the populace today, I reminded him.

"If everyone, including eventually the family cat and dog, sets up a separate ménage, I suppose you feel the divorce rate will be lowered? The fact that landlords will be the only ones left with an income I suppose doesn't matter?"

He had a nice laugh, only faintly tinged with male condescension, and for some reason I felt encouraged.

"It's an individual test for each one who takes part," I said. "If you don't believe in the testimony of the past, the present will perhaps confirm your disbelief. On the other hand, it may raise questions in your mind. For all anyone knows, the old way of group living may return. If you look at it closely, I'm sure you'll think it is at least worth a try."

He asked again to be reassured on several points. It must be understood that no change would be made in his office hours; that if he agreed to be "assimilated" into the family circle he would have one night a week free for his own diversions; and that nothing, but nothing, would be expected of him beyond the agreement to serve one year. His choice of verb made it sound like penal servitude, and perhaps he had a shadowy suggestion of that in his mind. His salary as "uncle" was to be paid to charity, he stipulated, and he named a home for elderly single men to be the beneficiary.

By the time we had everything worked out I was a nervous wreck, and could only be grateful that Miss Mary had not persisted in her original plan to have two uncles. *Three* aunts, I told Phyllis, could not possibly be as exhausting as one uncle. Phyllis was upset because Uncle Reade, as she immediately designated him, could still keep up his own work while Aunt Victoria must not work outside the home. The whole purpose of Miss Mary's idea, I tried to explain, was to create the old pattern, in which women did not go to business but spent their time (or so I had been told) heaping wood on the home fires to keep them burning brightly. Phyllis sniffed and dismissed the theoretical fire tenders as "dopes."

The capture of Uncle Reade, as Phyllis put it, completed the family, except for the children, and Miss Mary assured us they would be ready as soon as the moving in was accomplished. It was her idea that we arrange a housewarming, to include a tour of the spic-and-span house followed by a dinner in a private room of one of the good hotels. Of course, she could not be persuaded to attend, but apparently she was having a wonderful time spending money.

The house was every woman's dream, and even the menfolk were enthusiastic over the plumbing fixtures, the abundance of electric outlets, and the heating plant. Why anyone should be fascinated by oil burners puzzled me, but Grandpa Lane, Father Hubbard, and Uncle Reade did everything but crawl inside the two monsters. When they could tear themselves away from this inspection they made a beeline for the garage, which was new and, to hear them tell it, far more important than any mere house could ever be. Ronnie Hubbard shared their excitement—he was saving to buy a car and was inordinately pleased that, according to his measurements, there would be room in the garage for it if he ever got it. A small secondhand car, he instructed me, required hardly any space at all.

I think he rather begrudged the three small, attractively decorated rooms on the fourth floor of the house that were set aside for the children. In imagination I'm sure he saw a small car neatly inserted in each room instead of the Price children. The interior decorator had done a good job—a blue-enameled bed, chest of drawers, and little table and chairs for Leila; the same in pink for Holly; and for Robert, oak. The twins were to be on this floor, too, and they had been encouraged to choose the colors and designs they preferred in wallpaper, curtains, and rugs. A stall shower and a bathroom had been fitted into an enormous old closet, an arrangement that had been repeated on two of the lower floors—as Jane Hubbard remarked to her mother, the closets were almost as large as some modern apartments.

If Ronnie thought cars should be comfortably housed before people, I'm sure Reade Coleman would have specified something exclusive on the roof for bachelors. He mellowed slightly when he found that he was to occupy a pleasant corner room on the third floor, with a smaller room attached that could be used as a study.

Jane Hubbard, who like her twin warmly supported Miss Mary's reasoning, reminded me gently that women also could possess inventive minds and that Aunt Victoria May might appreciate a little extra study space. She and Victoria were delighted to find the bachelor bedroom and study duplicated at the other end of the long hall. The color scheme, gray and white, had been chosen by Victoria, but she was surprised and delighted to find a desk and a typewriter in her new study. In fact, we had to drag her away from the machine that night, or she would have sat down and gone to work on her book immediately.

There were two other rooms on this floor, nicely furnished but smaller and not as light as the two corner rooms. These were for the live-in maids, Mrs. Hubbard had been told.

"If we have them," she said doubtfully. "How much outside help will be needed still hasn't been decided."

The Hubbards, father and mother, and Grandpa and Grandma Lane were pleased with their large, pleasant rooms and private baths on the second floor. Everything was freshly painted and papered, and there were plenty of the enormous closets that must have been a fetish with the builder, or his wife.

"This is the first time in my life," I overheard Grandma Lane say to Mother Hubbard, "that I've ever had enough closet space."

And not only Mother Hubbard fervently agreed with her, but Victoria May also murmured an assent.

The twins were more interested in the main floor, divided by the wide, graceful flight of stairs. On one side was the living room, with an old-fashioned square piano that startled the twins, who had never seen one. It was a museum piece, I explained, but beautifully preserved and expertly tuned. The room was so long that a television set and a large radio, placed at the far end, did not disturb the harmony created by the beautiful old-fashioned pieces of mahogany. A fire had been laid in the white-stone fireplace, but was not lighted. Heavy rose-colored silk damask curtains, floor length, over elaborately patterned lace curtains, hung at the windows, three at the front, two on the side wall.

Across the hall were two connecting rooms, the first rather formally furnished, the second and larger one a dining room. The furniture was mahogany (I found myself calculating how many hours of a woman's time it would take to rub all the mahogany in this house with lemon oil), the usual conventional pieces, with a round table that looked as if it could seat a dozen comfortably.

Linens and silver were in a lowboy, and while Grandma Lane and Mother Hubbard were exclaiming ecstatically over Irish linen and sterling silver, the men reached the kitchen. The twins and Victoria were nowhere in sight, but their muffled voices could be heard from the direction of the cellar.

"What's going on down there?" Reade Coleman demanded, unconsciously giving an excellent performance of a no-nonsense uncle.

He jerked open the door of the cellar stairway, and Jane Hubbard giggled happily.

"It's just too perfect," she said, as one voicing absolute content.

Victoria May came to the foot of the steps, and I peered around Father Hubbard to see her holding what looked like a glass jar between her two hands.

"It's peach preserve," she explained kindly to the three men. "Put up fifty years ago, according to the label."

"Spoiled long ago." Reade Coleman sounded as disgusted as he looked.

"Not necessarily," Victoria informed him. "I've read of food being buried in Egyptian tombs for ages and perfectly fresh when opened."

Grandma Lane and Mother Hubbard, hearing voices, had come out into the kitchen and had listened to this speech with mounting horror. Speaking together, they warned Victoria and the twins of the dangers of botulism and insisted that the jar be disposed of unopened. This, the twins argued, might expose innocent but ignorant finders to grave danger. It was their duty to make sure about the contents of the jar and safeguard the public. (This last statement was, of course, Victoria's.)

Ronnie made one last attempt to be what he termed "scientific." Would I, he appealed to me, assure his mother that one small taste of the preserve could not possibly harm him? He wanted to write up a school report—this was a marvelous opportunity!—and certainly a quick taste of the peach preserve could do him no harm.

"He'll spit it out," Victoria promised cheerfully, but then, as Elizabeth Hubbard reminded her, Ronnie was not her son.

As it happened, the question was settled suddenly and dramatically without further argument. The jar in Victoria's hand burst with a violence all out of proportion to its size. There was one loud crack, Victoria stepped back just in time to avoid a deluge and the most terrible odor filled the air. The twins went into action, each seizing an arm of Victoria's, and rushed her up the cellar stairs into the kitchen. Grandma Lane slammed the door, and then, and not until then, Ronnie ejaculated, "Whew!"

All this had taken so much time that if we were to keep the dinner reservation we would have to postpone the round-table discussion we had planned, either until after the meal or until another night. Grandma Lane suggested that we return to the house that same evening, and I seconded her motion. The men, she said, would be in a much more sensible mood after a good dinner. Hers was the voice of experience, and whether it was the excellent food or the superlative coffee (Miss Mary had stipulated no wine because, she said, she respected the Lanes' principles: Myrtle's dearly loved brother, we learned later, had died an alcoholic in his early twenties) the atmosphere became decidedly more relaxed.

I thought I should disappear once the guests had returned to

44

the house, but I was urged so cordially to sit in at the round-table discussion that I could hardly refuse. The twins seemed especially anxious for my presence, and when we were finally seated at the table in the dining room I found Ronnie on my right and Jane on my left. I wondered a little at the apparent intensity of their interest, but the reason was promptly supplied.

Grandpa Lane said, with the little preliminary cough that seems characteristic of the speaker who addresses an audience, "I believe we are assembled here tonight to discuss the division of—er—duties."

Jane nudged me, and Ronnie muttered something that sounded like "This is going to be good."

I noticed that, perhaps instinctively, they were seated in the more-or-less conventional "family" order, the Lanes representing the head and foot of the table, the Hubbards to their right and left, Victoria May on one side, Reade Coleman facing her. The twins, too, I hoped, would ordinarily be separated by the width of the table, in the interest of peace and decorum.

"Well, I should think an issue of the greatest importance would be—er—the cooking," Reade Coleman suggested, glancing at Father Hubbard, who flashed him instant if wordless support.

"The cooking!" Beside me Jane bounced indignantly.

"You're here only because you agreed to keep still," her father reminded her. "One more interruption and out you go."

My sympathies were with Jane—probably for at least sixteen of the seventeen years of her life her slightest attempt to speak had been listened to and encouraged. I glanced at Ronnie. He, too, had sustained a shock, I judged, but he was enjoying the effect on Jane.

"I've been wondering about that." Mrs. Hubbard spoke

quickly. "I simply can't stand having anyone in the kitchen when I'm cooking. It makes me nervous. And usually when it's time to clear up there's never anyone around."

Victoria May was ruffling her hair into spikes and gave a front lock a vigorous yank as she burst into speech. "I'm sorry, but you can't count on me for cooking. I can heat up a TV dinner, and that's it. Perhaps it's because food doesn't interest me."

"I don't want anyone in my kitchen when I'm cooking, either," Grandma Lane said in a placid voice. Her black frock had a mauve vestee today, and her white hair, shampooed and beautifully set that afternoon, looked lovely. Her blue eyes surveyed us serenely through silver-rimmed spectacles. "It stands to reason two women will get in each other's way. But we could take turns—Elizabeth Hubbard one week, me the next. That might be fair."

Since no one dissented, the question was dismissed as settled. Victoria May, serving as secretary (Ronnie had labeled her "scorekeeper"), made an entry in her little book and announced that she wished to make a suggestion.

"The twins are going on eighteen—they were seventeen last fall," she announced. "They're old enough to be useful."

She spoke so matter-of-factly and by her manner so completely managed to ignore the presence of Ronnie and Jane that even they were too startled to attempt to defend themselves.

"I think they could set the table and clear it after meals," Victoria continued, still in that curiously detached manner. "And let them operate the dishwasher. There will be plenty of errands they can do, too, of course."

"We have to go to school," Ronnie muttered before I could hush him.

He was informed that he would have plenty of time to go to

school and all his evenings would be free for studying. Neither Ronnie nor his sister brightened perceptibly at this reminder.

"Perhaps Jane would like to ask a question," Grandpa Lane suggested when Victoria paused, perhaps for breath.

"Well, what I'd like to know is," Jane declared with no hesitation, "what are the men going to do?"

"A very good question," Victoria said graciously, and I thought so myself.

Grandpa Lane announced, in a tone of dignified reproof, that he intended to plant and care for an extensive vegetable garden. Yes, he admitted, March was not the time to start a garden, but a good deal could be done to get the ground ready, and he could also be planning the layout of the garden on paper.

"You're always the first one up," his wife reminded him. "So you could fetch the newspaper, unless it's delivered. And with the children in school there'll be errands to be done during the day."

She spoke as one quite accustomed to planning her husband's time, and I for one had no doubt that, with three women in the house, the old gentleman would be provided with plenty of occupation.

Miles Hubbard evidently had been briefed by Miss Mary, for now he quietly announced that he was prepared to keep the household accounts and handle the cash disbursements. Once a bookkeeper, always a bookkeeper, he said, and smiled—a little wryly, I thought. But his air of quiet efficiency inspired confidence. Not for the first time, it occurred to me that if Miss Mary's wild experiment really jelled and turned out to be a success, a great deal might be owed to the personality of this quiet man. He might lack imagination—heaven knew we had plenty of that—but he was intelligent and he had common sense.

Reade Coleman, silent up to this moment, suddenly came to. He had been waiting to hear, he told us blandly, about Miss May's contribution to the household as planned.

"I understand the agreement calls for her to resign her job—her position—outside the—er—home."

Mrs. Hubbard consulted a list of typewritten notes.

"You're to make the beds, Victoria," she said. "And generally straighten up the rooms every morning. All of us, Mrs. Lane and you and me, can share the daily dusting and light vacuuming."

She added that a woman had been engaged to come in three days a week to clean and do odd jobs. If necessary she could be engaged for five days a week.

"And Mr. Coleman—I must get used to calling you Reade, I suppose—well, there are what I call 'stepladder jobs,' you know. You are so active and tall that I'm sure you'll be a wonderful help."

Reade Coleman's look of apprehension was ludicrous, but she cheerfully ignored it. He would be *such* a help, she told him, when it came to hanging curtains, putting up rods, or inserting bulbs in ceiling lights. And of course a man was always needed when it was necessary to move a heavy piece of furniture.

"And then there are the children," she finished, almost airily.

Reade's apprehensive look became a horrified stare.

"What—what about the children?" he gasped.

"The Price children, you know." Mrs. Hubbard was soothing. "Robert, Leila, and Holly. Naturally you'll want to take them to the zoo and other educational places."

Beside me, Ronnie jerked convulsively, but he managed to keep quiet. Jane simply stared at Reade, her mouth open.

"Why me? Why me?" Reade was demanding. "I don't know

them, they don't know me. Aren't there enough women around to look after these brats—I mean kids—er—children—without getting me involved?"

Suddenly his wild gaze focused on the twins.

"Why can't they do it?" he shouted. "Two of them. Let them go to the zoo! Why not?"

Victoria was enjoying every minute of this, and it was her increasing hilarity that finally helped to restore Reade's self-control. All he asked, he said hoarsely, was to learn the reason why he should be expected to be involved in any plan remotely connected with children.

Mrs. Hubbard, who had waited patiently for him to subside, suggested he might like a glass of water. What the man needed, I thought, was a shot of bourbon, and I hoped Mr. Hubbard would see that he got it later.

"One of Miss Mary's happiest memories," said Mrs. Hubbard, when Reade finally seemed to be breathing normally, "is of being taken to the zoo as a child. And on excursions. Her mother's unmarried brother was perfectly devoted to her, and she wants to re-create a similar relationship for the three Price children."

Her explanation, however kindly meant, served only to deepen Reade Coleman's horror. He felt trapped, but he would not break the year's agreement, even though at that moment the twelve months ahead must have seemed like an eternity.

"We shall all have to make adjustments," Mrs. Lane's soft voice consoled him. "Once we have adapted—"

The meeting, discussion, call it by any other name and the aftereffects would have been the same, was ended by the announcement from Mr. Hubbard that I would be glad to listen to suggestions and/or complaints. This explained the warmth of the invitation extended to me to "sit in" at the first round-table discussion, but I felt that I should have at least been left a loophole for escape.

Mr. Lane—it was going to be easy to call him "Grandpa"—managed to haul himself to his feet by grasping the edge of the table. He had a question he'd like settled, he mumbled, fixing his gaze on me. "What about the scuttle coal?" he asked severely.

"What *is* scuttle coal?" I whispered to Ronnie, who promptly informed me, in a perfectly audible voice, that scuttle coal was coal carried in a scuttle to replenish small fires.

"There's a good gas range in the kitchen, and a 'lectric stove, too," the old man enumerated. "Why's anyone need a coal stove? Carrying coal up those cellar steps is enough to break your back—and for no good reason."

He seemed to have forgotten his first raptures about coal stoves. His wife's serene expression did not change, but Jane Hubbard pushed back her chair and stood up.

"A coal fire is good for lots of things," she said instructively. "You can make super toast over red-hot coals. Anyway, we won't need a fire in the coal stove unless the gas or electricity gives out. Right?"

He believed in getting things settled before the last minute, the old man muttered; he always wanted to know where he stood. Ronnie, stifling a laugh, coughed and then choked, and Grandpa Lane, after one suspicious glance at him, sat down.

Victoria May stood up, as economical of movement as of words.

"What about the bathrooms?" she asked.

There would be no problem, Mrs. Hubbard thought, if each member of the family remembered to leave the tub or shower in the same good order in which he had found it. The cleaning woman could also be counted on to supervise.

Jane waited a moment, but no one said anything, so she stood up and, after an uneasy glance at her mother, announced that she and Ronnie would like to have the question of laundry settled.

"Oh, I ought to have known!" Mrs. Hubbard's laugh was rueful. "They wash and iron incessantly," she explained to us. "I suppose we'll have to devise some rules for the use of the laundry equipment."

Jane was saying that she didn't want to be unfair, but that she and Ronnie had to look after some of the school "things," as well as their own equipment, not to mention their clothes.

"I can iron better than my mother," she stated, not at all boastfully, simply as one stating a proved fact. "So I do some of the family ironing, too. Don't I, Moms?"

"You certainly do!" her mother assented warmly. "I try to think of that when it seems to me that you and Ronnie all but live in the laundry room. With this new, up-to-date equipment, I don't expect to see you except when you run out of detergent."

The laundry equipment in the light, dry cellar of the renovated house was certainly enough to fascinate any domestic-minded woman. I could understand how Grandma Lane felt when she said to me that if she were forty years younger she would be tempted to "take in washing" simply for the pleasure of using this expensive collection of the modern plumber's art. I may not have been quite as enthusiastic, but there was certainly a lot to be said for the inventor, or inventors, who had rescued women from the washboard and done it so thoroughly.

Not that Jane Hubbard's generation was satisfied. What every home needed, she had told me once, was a complete dry-cleaning "works," and now she disclosed that she had been taking notes, although she complained that the Acton dry-cleaning establishments had not been exactly co-operative. The ones she had interviewed, Jane said, had been suspicious.

"I tried to explain that we wouldn't do any dry cleaning for anyone outside the family," she told us earnestly. "But they all have the idea I might take business away from them. About all I learned is that fire insurance would be very expensive."

Her father, who had been in a state of shock—at least, I so interpreted his expression—appeared to relax.

"You're always saying how high the dry-cleaning bills are," Jane reminded him. "I should think you'd be interested when I try to save the family money."

"Cold water and a sponge—" Grandma Lane was prepared to give her recipe for the removal of spots, but Reade Coleman stirred impatiently, and (true to her generation, Victoria May whispered to me) automatically she yielded the floor to him.

"When we went out for dinner this evening, I left my *Evening Globe* on the hall table," Reade said, his voice and expression grim. "Now I find something's been cut out of it, before I even had a chance to read it. If there's one thing I can't stand, it's having my paper messed up before I read it."

Grandma Lane coughed apologetically.

"There was a recipe for a new kind of layer cake," she said. "Made with only three eggs. I clipped it out. I didn't think you'd mind."

Judging from his scowl Reade minded very much, but he mumbled something that Grandma Lane assumed to be conciliatory. Victoria seized the moment to announce that she wanted it thoroughly understood that no one, but no one, was to touch her typewriter but herself.

"I'd like to lock up my room whenever I leave it," she told us. "But then Bertha couldn't get in when she comes to clean. I simply can't risk any tampering with my machine, and with three children in the house—"

"They're not going to run wild," Mrs. Hubbard assured her. "They'll learn there are certain things that don't belong to them and certain rooms into which they must not go without an invitation or special permission. You needn't worry, Victoria."

Victoria looked far from convinced, and later I overheard her tell Reade that the keynote of modern child training was permissiveness and that she predicted constant trouble.

The twins, once they were fairly sure the laundry question was settled to their satisfaction, seemed content with the role of listeners, but an apparently casual remark from Grandpa Lane aroused them to passionate protest.

Their mother, in all good faith, had suggested that she thought the task of preparing meals would be made easier for Grandma Lane and herself if they first obtained some idea of the likes and dislikes of the family. Not, she hurriedly interpolated, that either cook should be expected to cater to individual palates—in a family of eleven, that wouldn't be practical—but it might be easier to adapt menus to the tastes of the majority if they had specific information.

Grandpa Lane hardly waited for her to finish before he was on his feet.

"Oysters!" he exclaimed, beaming upon the faces turned to him. "You can't go wrong if you serve oysters. Raw, broiled, baked, fried—there isn't anything you can't do with oysters. And they're full of vitamins or something, too. Give me a plate of raw oysters three times a week and I won't ask for anything better."

In the startled silence that followed this impassioned outburst, Ronnie's whisper to Jane sounded clear and distinct.

"He can have 'em, along with snails," Ronnie said, and Jane shuddered.

"Nasty, slimy things—they make me sick," she whispered. "I'll die if we have to have them three times a week."

She subsided at a glance from her father, but I gathered from the lack of enthusiasm that oysters were not the favorite food of anyone except Grandpa. And the same might be inferred from the silence that greeted Victoria May's utterance of the word "salad."

"Everyone should have salad twice a day," she declared brightly. "The variety is infinite and so are the dressings. I can easily make a meal of salad, and for growing children the benefits are incalculable."

Reade Coleman didn't exactly shudder, but he looked alarmed. His suggestion was that a good roast of beef, varied with roast lamb and, at intervals, roast chicken or turkey, would be economical as well as good eating. He was quite ready to present a lecture on the merits of roasting or broiling meat as opposed to frying it, but Grandma Lane interrupted him. Did he, she asked sweetly, know how to carve a roast of beef?

Reade admitted that he had never tried his hand at carving anything, but he was quite sure that all that was needed was a good knife. Women, he added gratuitously, never paid enough attention to the importance of good carving equipment. He had been a guest at countless dinner tables where the struggles of the host to cut even the wing off a bird were painful to watch.

"Suppose we ask Mrs. Lane her preferences," Mr. Hubbard suggested. "One I'm fairly sure of—good coffee. Am I right?"

She smiled at him contentedly. "Nothing can compare with really good coffee, to my way of thinking," she said. "I drink it three times a day, although Caspar thinks that's too often."

Mrs. Hubbard confided that two cups of coffee at breakfast was her daily quota and that she thought roasts were rather wasteful except for large families.

"I keep forgetting that we *are* a large family." She smiled. "However, I'll keep my recipe for meat loaf handy, just in case we have the problem of leftovers."

"Meat loaf is nothing but hash," Reade Coleman said,

rather rudely, but he quickly apologized. "I suppose it depends on who makes it."

Jane Hubbard was instantly on her feet.

"My mother's meat loaf is nothing like hash!" she blazed at the astonished Reade. "It's perfectly delicious. People at our church suppers always ask if they can count on getting Mom's meat loaf."

Her mother said, "Don't get so excited, darling," and Jane sat down.

"I was speaking of the ordinary variety of meat loaf," Reade Coleman assured her. "I've never tasted your mother's."

Jane still looked ruffled, and her mother was evidently relieved when Victoria reminded her that so far the twins had expressed no preferences. As for the three children, they would most likely vote for animal crackers and milk—that had been her favorite food combination at their age, she said.

"Angel-food cake is mine," Jane admitted. "No icing, just lots of cake. But I don't suppose we could have that every day, could we?"

Her mother thought it unlikely, and Ronnie's choice, baked beans, was not exactly a dish to have every day, either. But all the suggestions had been helpful, she assured them, and everyone could expect to find his or her choice served as frequently as possible.

"Even oysters?" Jane demanded.

"Even oysters," her mother answered.

Part Two

The Family

5

"More coffee, anyone?" Elizabeth Hubbard, four weeks later, beamed hospitably at the faces turned toward her. "It's such a beautiful day," she added, dispensing cheer as well as the breakfast beverage.

Only the twins declined a second cup—Reade Coleman found their preference for what he termed "beakers" of cold milk depressing—and after the little flurry of passing cups, the sugar bowl, and the cream pitcher silence again enveloped the breakfast table.

Elizabeth looked at her husband reproachfully. She supposed he missed his old habit of reading his morning paper— the headlines at least—during breakfast; but if he read his paper now, Grandpa Lane and Reade Coleman would probably follow his example, and three newspaper readers at one table were really more than any womenfolk should be asked to endure. Why should it be so difficult, Elizabeth thought desperately, to *talk?* Granted that they were not completely adjusted—that was the twins' favorite word—to each other yet, surely in the three weeks they had been together they must have developed some points of common interest.

She looked at Grandpa Lane, apparently absorbed in picking the raisins out of a large, fluffy bun, heedless of his wife's frowning disapproval. Victoria May was stirring her coffee absent-mindedly, like one withdrawn from the earthly plane. Elizabeth rather envied her such evident ability to remain detached. There were plenty of times when she herself would have liked to retreat from communication with a demanding world. Only, of course, there were always the twins. She glanced affectionately at Jane and Ronnie, seated (for obvious reasons) on opposite sides of the table. It was Saturday, and doubtless they had their day already planned. She wondered a little at their patience with the prolonged breakfast. Ordinarily they would, she thought, have been eager to be up and away. The children, Robert and Leila and Holly, had been dismissed twenty minutes ago—it was hardly fair to expect them to sit quietly once they had finished their oatmeal. *Why doesn't someone say something?*

"It's the first sunny Saturday we've had in three weeks," Victoria May said.

Before anyone could respond to this announcement, three small figures pranced into the dining room. They were variously attired in garments obviously not their own. Robert, as befitted the dignity of the only boy, carried a cane, and the scarf he had wound around his neck was so long that he ran the risk of choking himself by stepping on it as he walked. His sisters were draped in tan-colored raincoats that dragged out behind them like trains. Each little girl carried a small red pocketbook dangling from a short chain.

"Aren't you through eating *yet?*" Robert demanded incredulously.

"We've been ready for hours and hours," Leila said, giving her pocketbook a carefree twirl.

Holly contented herself with flashing a devastating smile and edging forward to extend her left hand, buried in a large wash-leather glove.

"That's my glove!" Reade Coleman pushed back his chair. "Just what do you kids think you are doing, anyway?" he demanded, stretching out one long arm, with the intention of snatching the glove.

Holly shrieked, an unnerving scream that startled everyone and possibly herself. She turned to run, tripped on the raincoat, and fell against Leila, who in turn nearly toppled Robert. All three of them, in a tangle, caromed against Reade Coleman's chair.

"What the—" He swallowed the next half-dozen words, but the effort nearly choked him. "What do you think you're doing?" he repeated when he could trust his voice.

Three small voices united to inform him.

"Zoo!" they shrieked happily. "We're going to the zoo."

Reade stared at them in horror, but Victoria helped herself to a piece of coffee cake and smiled.

"It's a beautiful day. I hope you have a lovely time," she said.

The small, compact Robert eyed Reade man to man.

"You said the first free Saturday, Uncle Reade," he reminded the visibly shaken man.

The fact that it had rained for the three previous Saturdays had lulled Reade into a trap of false security. Some weather bureau, somewhere, he was even now frantically reminding

61

himself, had statistics to prove that the number of stormy Saturdays in a year exceeded the fair readings by a substantial majority. And certainly any man who played golf would go along with that. It was undoubtedly pouring cats and dogs in all other sections of the country this morning—

"I wouldn't count on the weather, Bobby," he told the boy. "It'll cloud up and we're likely to have rain any moment now. You can't enjoy the animals in the zoo gardens when it's raining."

The complete silence that greeted his remarks was worse than a barrage of arguments.

Leila's little voice, grave and sweet, broke the tension.

"You always keep your word, you know, Uncle Reade." She looked at him steadily. "You told us you always keep your word."

"I don't have my car this weekend. I left it yesterday to have the brakes relined." He looked hopefully at the silent, watchful faces surrounding him: only Grandma Lane looked as if she might be sympathetic, had she known what to do—or say.

"It's perfectly easy to get there by bus," Victoria volunteered. Trust her to add to his troubles!

"Take my advice and get a good start," Miles Hubbard advised, folding his napkin. "Children tire easily. You won't have to put in a full day—nowhere near it. Coming, Ronnie?"

"I'll get them put together for you," Jane offered, as everyone left the table. "Give me fifteen minutes, and we'll meet you in the front hall."

Reade looked at her with mixed admiration and exasperation. She ought to be taking the kids to the zoo, since evidently she had a way with them. For all he knew, she would *enjoy* the trip. A woman ought to be on hand to manage the two little girls, at least. His feeling of desperation—that he had been thrown to the wolves, so to speak—was intensified by the sight of Leila descending the hall stairway, neatly attired in a buttoned brown coat and brown socks and shoes. Her straight shining hair had been brushed, and she carried a pair of diminutive white gloves.

"I'm a lady," she announced, pausing to admire herself in the hall mirror. "I'm wearing my yellow chambray under this coat."

"You look very nice," he assured her, and tilted the mirror slightly so that she could see herself full length.

"I hope you don't mind that I'm not wearing earrings," she confided, smiling approval of herself in the glass.

Robert, brushed and combed and decently arrayed, shot down the banisters in time to hear.

"Earrings!" he repeated. "You haven't got any earrings. Nobody wears earrings until they're grown up."

"You don't know anything about it—you're only a boy!" Leila, with superb disdain, seated herself on the hall bench.

Victoria May came out into the hall, and glanced at the open door of the coat closet and the raincoats in an untidy heap on the floor. "If the children pulled those coats off the hangers, is there any reason why they shouldn't put them back again?"

Reade muttered something to the effect that he didn't have all day. "Come on, kids, what are we waiting for? I thought you wanted to go to the zoo."

He turned to open the street door when Jane's clear voice halted him. She was beginning the descent of the stairs, holding Holly by one hand.

"Unkie, you're short a customer," she reminded Reade. "You'll have to keep track better than this, or you're liable to wind up short at the end of the day."

Holly, who in a red coat and cap resembled a plump little robin, eyed Reade severely. "Bad man," she remarked, but without animosity.

"That's her word for the day," Jane explained. "She gets fascinated with a word and applies it to everything. Don't pay any attention—she probably adores you in her secret heart."

Victoria pointed to the tangle of raincoats on the closet floor. "First things first," she said. "Pick up the coats, and then you'll be ready for a lovely treat."

"The coats can wait!" Reade wrenched the door open, almost knocking over Leila, who had surreptitiously been trying to turn the knob. "If we're going to the zoo, for God's sake, let's go to the zoo!"

Jane laughed, a shocked Victoria admonished him to watch his language, and at last they were off. The bus stop, two blocks from the house, might have been two miles, an exasperated Reade fumed, considering the time it took his party to walk to it. Robert was determined to investigate the gutter, Leila was intent on adopting a stray cat, and Holly found the trash baskets of absorbing interest.

"I thought you wanted to go to the zoo!" Reade reminded them endlessly. "If you just want to take a walk, say so and we can be home in time for lunch."

He should have known better than to mention lunch, he told himself bitterly, when the three small voices complained of sudden hunger. "Let's run for the bus," he suggested, hoping to create a diversion. Taking Holly by the hand, he allowed the two others to race ahead, Leila screaming for Robert to wait for her.

On any other day, the exasperated Reade thought, they would have had to wait ten or fifteen minutes for the bus, always operating on an erratic schedule. Not this time! As the small, flying figures tore down the street, shrieking wildly, the long, bright green bus pulled up at the stop.

"Wait for my uncle!" Leila was imploring the driver when Reade reached them.

Robert scrambled into the bus, and Leila, ignoring Reade's

command to wait until he could help her, wriggled up the steps on all fours. A row of interested adult faces surveyed Reade through the windows as he lifted up Holly. "In you go," he assured her, with what he hoped was a reasonable facsimile of cheerfulness.

To his horror, Holly began to scream. She not only screamed; she also kicked and clawed. Her red hat fell off and was retrieved by a fascinated passer-by, who stood holding it and beaming idiotically.

"No! No!" shrieked Holly, beginning to sob, great heart-rending sobs, the pitiful protest of a helpless child.

Robert, who had found himself a seat in the bus, returned to eye his sister coldly.

"Most of the time she likes riding in a bus," he observed, to no one in particular. "This is one time she doesn't."

An elderly woman, seated near the door, murmured that some people shouldn't attempt to handle children. It was a matter of insight, and you take her son-in-law—

Leila had propped herself up against the frowning bus driver.

"Why do we have to wait for her?" she murmured crossly.

"Shut the door! It's freezing in here," someone in the back of the bus protested. "Get going. Never mind the kid, get going."

"Mister, I can't wait all day," said the bus driver, speaking for the first time.

The harassed Reade glared impartially at his audience. "Get off, you two," he ordered, keeping a firm grip on the sobbing Holly.

"Leila's afraid to get off," Robert informed him. "She might fall."

Reade and the bus driver muttered something simultaneously, and the elderly woman voiced her opinion of persons who used profanity within the hearing of innocent children.

"Oh, I know some swear words," Robert assured her kindly. "Would you like to hear me—"

"You get off this bus now—immediately—at once." Reade gritted, his teeth clenched. "Never mind helping Leila. You get *off*!"

Robert tumbled down the steps, and Leila began to cry. She didn't want to stay alone on the nasty old bus. "Make Robert come back!" she wailed.

"Oh, for God's sake!" The bus driver eased himself out of his seat, picked up the now screaming child, and swung her, not ungently, to the curb. It was doubtful if he heard the chorus that chanted "Good-bye" and "Thank you" as he drove away.

The day was unseasonably cold, and in spite of the sunshine Holly was shivering. They were at least a mile from the zoo and would be facing the wind. Walking was out of the question, Reade decided, and as he hailed a taxi he told himself that he was prepared to stuff the children into it by main force. They looked half frozen, and if they came down with colds he would never hear the end of it.

The cab slid to a stop, and Reade, momentarily releasing his grip on Holly, opened the door. She instantly darted around him and plunged into the shabby, comfortable depths of the interior. Leila followed her example, but this time it was Robert who held back.

"I think I'd rather walk," he said politely.

To Reade's expostulations—that it was more than a mile to the zoo, that the wind was increasing, that he could easily lose his way—the boy made no reply. The cabbie, his meter ticking merrily, looked interested but aloof.

"You needn't wait for me," Robert told him grandly. "I like to walk. The girls get tired, but I don't."

"You do so get tired!" Leila declared, from inside the cab.

Reade's waning patience abruptly snapped.

"Get into that cab and shut up!" he barked, seizing the boy by the coat collar. "I've had just about enough of this nonsense. Get in, I tell you—get in!"

Robert bellowed, twisting and turning, but he was no match for his captor, who dumped him headfirst into the cab, to the delight of the little girls, whose giggles were as unnerving as Robert's yells.

"What's the matter with him?" The cabbie twisted about to get a better view of his recalcitrant passenger.

Reade had little breath left for explanations, but his muttered "Get going" had an unfortunate effect.

"You the kid's father?" the driver asked, suspicion beginning to dominate curiosity.

Robert was now screaming "Help! Help!" and a crowd was collecting on the curb. A man cried, "Here comes a cop!" and a woman cooed, with sickening sweetness, "Poor lamb! Is the bad man taking you away from your mommy?"

"I want my mommy!" screamed Robert, aiming a kick at Reade's face and narrowly missing him.

"What goes on here?" inquired the voice of the law, behind Reade's back. "Somebody hurt?"

"It's a kidnap," a woman on the edge of the crowd announced positively. "The poor little kid. Imagine his mother—"

Reade, who had been halfway in the cab and halfway out, straightened up to face the officer. The three children were silent.

"Your kids?" the policeman asked politely.

"Not exactly." Reade pulled at his tie, which had worked its way around under one ear. "That is, I'm responsible for them, but I'm no blood relation. We're going to the zoo."

". . . probably cruel to them," a whisper drifted from the fascinated onlookers. "Personally, I never trust these smiling men."

"To the zoo? You mean they're upset about going to the zoo?" The policeman stooped to look in at the children, now huddled together in a corner of the seat. They stared at him, obviously frightened. The cab driver managed, simply by the set of his shoulders, to imply a neutral attitude.

Reade had opened his wallet and taken out a card. For a moment he hesitated, surveying the crowd with frank distaste.

"My personal card would mean little or nothing to you," he said to the waiting officer. "But the name of my—my employer may carry weight. A phone call to her office will provide verification."

He offered the card, and for a moment the officer studied it in silence. He glanced from the cab to Reade, clearly bewildered.

"Miss Mary Hall?" He glanced again at the card in his hand before returning it to Reade. "Of course I've heard of her. But these kids don't belong to her, do they? She hasn't got a family, far as I know."

But enough of the details of Miss Mary's latest experiment had filtered through to the various city departments to furnish the police with a sketchy print of her latest activity. It was something to do with families, the thread of the story ran, and children would be the natural concern.

"I always thought kids liked to go to the zoo," said Officer Layor, in a last desperate attempt to make sense out of this incident. "Times must have changed since I was their age."

"You don't realize the half of it," Reade assured him, and hoped that he hadn't closed the cab door with too much emphasis.

The zoo finally reached, Reade glanced at the children in some dismay. They looked unaccountably untidy, yet they had started out that morning with hair shining, faces clean, and clothing neat and trim. Now Holly looked as though she had been mopping up the floor of the cab, and not only was Robert's coat unbuttoned, but his shirt as well—if he came down with a cold, Mrs. Hubbard would probably blame him, Reade thought.

"Well, what shall we see first?" he asked cheerily, hustling his charges toward the building nearest the gates.

Leila had evidently made up her mind during the trip.

"First the monkeys, then the lions, then the zebra," she said.

Robert sneezed. "I want to eat first," he announced.

"Button your shirt," Reade commanded. "*And* your coat. Holly, what do you want to see? Girls," he hastily reminded Robert, "should have first choice."

Holly's blue eyes turned to him anxiously. "I want to go to the bathroom, please," she said.

Reade's dismay, reflected in his face, was correctly interpreted by Leila.

Holly, she confided, always wanted to go to the bathroom. "I can take her. You wait for us," she directed, with a motherly air that was oddly reassuring.

She was not disconcerted when he pointed out that she didn't know where the rest rooms were. "You ask people," she told him.

A sympathetic guard in the first building they came to supplied the information, and Leila and Holly disappeared down a gloomy corridor. They were gone for what seemed an unconscionable length of time to the waiting Reade, who found himself recalling horrific and long-forgotten news stories of assaults upon innocent children, and when they finally returned his tormented nerves found relief in a display of authority.

"I've had enough of this!" he snapped at the startled youngsters. "We'll see the monkeys and then the lions, and no one is to straggle along. Keep close together and behave yourselves."

Holly flashed him an enchanting smile. "I'm hungry, Unkie," she said.

No one was hungry at half past ten in the morning, he told her, resisting the charm of that smile. They would see the animals and then have a nice hot lunch—

"A hot dog," Robert interposed, pointing to the gaily fluttering flags on an approaching cart.

"Ice cream cone," Leila suggested, and Holly specified, "Stromberry with choc'late."

A man with a small boy in tow passed them, the child holding a frankfurter and roll from which a generous fringe of mustard dripped. The two men exchanged glances, and the stranger muttered sheepishly.

"What did he say, Unkie?" Leila asked.

Before Reade could open his mouth, Robert answered.

" 'If you can't beat 'em, join 'em,' " he reported, frowning a little. "I suppose he meant something."

"I'll make a bargain with you," Reade said in desperation. "If you each have a—a hot dog now, you won't ask for anything more to eat until we have lunch. How about that?"

They agreed enthusiastically, and the vendor greeted them with a lavish display of words and unlimited quantities of mustard. Each child politely offered Reade a "first bite" of the delicacy, a gesture that surprised and touched him. But as they trudged toward the zoo buildings he was surprised to see that they were holding their buns carefully in the paper napkins and not eating at all.

"What's the matter? Isn't it good?" he asked Robert. "I thought you were faint from hunger, and suddenly you've all lost interest."

"We're saving them," Robert said matter-of-factly.

Leila and Holly nodded, but did not speak.

"Saving them!" Reade stared at the trio. "What are you saving them *for?*"

Robert stopped to tuck the paper napkin more securely around his bun. He sighed as if weary of explaining the obvious.

"To eat in the lion house," he said. "But Leila wants to eat hers when we see the monkeys, and Holly—"

Reade interrupted, his tone savage. "You eat those things here and now. Eat them now, or throw them away. Hear me?"

He could be heard a block away. Fortunately, except for the vendor, now several yards behind them, no one else was in sight. Some sixth sense must have warned Reade's tormentors that the limits of his endurance had been reached, for they hurriedly, silently, and vigorously began to munch. Reade waited in ominous silence while they eyed him furtively. Had he been able to appreciate the humorous side of the situation, he might have laughed at the picture presented by the three small figures standing stiffly before him, small mouths chomping steadily but without enjoyment.

Leila and Robert went through the motions of mopping each other and then Holly with the crumpled napkins, and Reade, already ashamed of his ill temper, found their new docility unbearably pathetic—after all, he wasn't a man to throw his weight around.

"Good!" He congratulated them heartily when Robert had disposed of the napkins in a litter basket. "Now we're ready for the sights. I think we're headed straight for the lion house. Let's go there first?"

The king of beasts apparently bored the children. Robert got into a shouting match with another small boy, in the charge of a nervous elderly woman identified as "Aunt Molly," who insisted that the lions were sensitive to raised voices and might try to escape from the cages. Leila developed a hitherto unsuspected fondness for snakes, and once in the snake house insisted on a prolonged tour, heedless of Holly's terrified wails and Robert's pretended boredom.

"They've seen them before," she said carelessly, when Reade remonstrated. "It won't hurt them to look around some more."

She, with Robert and Holly, visited the zoo every year, Leila told a perplexed Reade. If their parents didn't take them a cousin of Daddy's usually did. And no one ever let her stay in the snake house long enough to enjoy herself, Leila complained.

"When I grow up, I won't be so selfish," she said, her lovely eyes brimming with sorrow.

Reade, who was finding himself unexpectedly mesmerized by the exhibits—he calculated it must have been thirty years since he had visited the zoo—wanted to have a second look at the magnificent Bengal tiger endlessly pacing the narrow oblong of his cage, but the increasing ennui of his charges made him hesitate to suggest a return visit to the lion house. As they left the snakes Leila sighed deeply.

"What Robert really wants to see," she confided, slipping a small hand into Reade's, "is a movie. I think it might be a good idea," she added, suddenly as sedate as an adult.

"I don't know why you want to go to a movie when we came to visit the zoo," Reade argued. In his way, he felt, he was as obstinate as the children, but, after all, the zoo trip had been their original suggestion.

Holly abruptly sat down on a trash box. "I want to see a movie," she crooned, rocking herself back and forth. "I'll kick and scream, I'll kick and scream—"

Reade discovered that what he wanted was to shake her until her small bones rattled, and the intensity of this violent desire shocked him so much that he found himself explaining, with elaborate patience, that the movies were too far away.

"Perhaps we can go tomorrow," he offered hopefully.

Holly pouted, and he turned to Leila, who was tugging at his sleeve. A popcorn vendor had halted on the other side of the path and appeared to be in a comfortable trance.

"Not until we have lunch!" Reade forestalled Leila's plea. "You'll enjoy it more this afternoon," he assured her.

Holly was not interested in popcorn. She had slipped down from the trash box and was now raising the lid, her expression that of the earnest explorer. Leila dashed forward and Reade called a warning.

"Look out for her fingers! Stop that, Holly!" He managed to catch the lid of the box before it fell on Holly's ungloved little hands.

"There's nothing but dirt in it." Leila consoled Holly, who had begun to cry, the tears dropping silently one by one. She looked unbearably fragile and pathetic.

"Never mind, we'll go have lunch—you'll like that, won't you?" Reade was beginning to feel the limitations of his communication with the young. "You be thinking what kind of ice cream you want for dessert."

Holly brightened, but Leila looked worried. She turned to Reade with the air of one who shared his responsibilities.

"I don't see Robert anywhere, do you?" she asked seriously.

Robert, indeed, was not to be seen. Reade's alarm was deepened by his inability to remember how long it had been since he *had* seen the boy. He had expected the three children to keep together. (For one wild moment he wondered whether he had been remiss in not insisting they be tied after the fashion of mountain climbers.) He gripped Holly firmly by the hand— that would be one who wouldn't get away!—and tried to smile reassuringly at Leila.

"I heard him say he was going to hide," she said, and when Reade asked where, she whispered, "In a bear's den."

"Oh, good grief!" Exasperated, Reade was also relieved.

73

"He can't hide in any bear den." Not, he admitted to himself, if there happened to be a bear in it. That Robert was capable of stowing himself away in any handy, safe place he did not doubt.

"I think he's in with a bear," Leila insisted, but she listened silently while Reade questioned a passing guard.

It was absolutely out of the question for a child to get into any of the bear dens unobserved, the guard declared. It had never happened, and he was willing to bet a week's pay that it hadn't happened now. Too many people about, and besides, there was an alarm system. This wasn't public knowledge, but a year or two ago a few "nuts" had had the bright idea of trying to photograph a hibernating bear.

No, the guard had not seen a wandering small boy, although every week a few kids got lost and wound up in the office to which distracted parents in search of them were directed. His best bet, Reade was told, was to go to the office and wait. "He'll turn up there sooner or later," the guard prophesied cheerfully.

"You're hurting my hand," Holly complained, and smiled forgivingly when Reade apologized. "Let's go see a bear. Why not?"

The guard had walked on, and Reade turned, intending to follow the path back to the office. He was just in time to see Leila pick up something from the ground and put it into her mouth.

"Leila!" He stared at the little girl in horror. "What are you eating? Spit it out—do you hear me? Spit it out!"

"Why?" She began to chew vigorously. "It's only popcorn," she explained.

Reade glared. Was she so starved, he demanded, that she had to pick up popcorn from the dirty ground? "What do you think you're doing?" he finished redundantly.

Leila glanced at him over her shoulder. She continued to

walk slowly, apparently studying the ground. Reade and Holly watched while she made a second darting forward movement and snatched up another piece of popcorn—if it was popcorn—from the gravel in the path. Instead of eating it, she held it out on the palm of her hand for Reade to see.

"It's popcorn," she said, in a tone of kind forbearance.

"I can see it's popcorn," Reade snapped. "What are you doing with it?"

He had an uneasy impression that she exchanged a look of secret comprehension with Holly before she answered.

"It's a trail, dear." Her voice imitated exactly Elizabeth Hubbard's inflection when restraining her impatience with an obtuse husband. "You know, Robert's trail. Like the Indians."

If this was perfectly clear to her, Reade required clarification. Where was Robert? And what Indians was she talking about?

Leila explained, while Holly regarded "Unkie" with the pity she evidently reserved for the hopelessly retarded. Robert had left a trail of popcorn for them to follow, Leila revealed. It was perfectly clean, good popcorn, and it had not been on the ground long enough to get dirty. She was finally persuaded to leave it for the birds—they would find it a delightful treat. Holly was disposed to linger and make sure not a kernel was wasted, but she trotted along amiably when reminded that birds were shy and did not like the company of people. Reade, who had only half believed the trail story—it seemed to him that Robert would be far more likely to eat the popcorn than to scatter it—was surprised to hear a confusion of voices as they rounded a turn and saw ahead of him a milling group of people whose excited voices produced an unintelligible clamor. Reade took a firm grip on Leila's hand and felt his other hand grasped more tightly by Holly.

They reached the group, but nothing could be seen of Robert, although Reade thought he heard his voice. The bodies, legs, and waving arms of the crowd made an effective screen, and for a moment Reade wondered if the child might not have been trampled upon. He caught the eye of a middle-aged man on the edge of the crowd, but the stranger, who said something in a foreign tongue, apparently knew no English.

"What goes on?" Reade, trying to push his way through the crowd, was hampered by the two small girls.

A woman heard his question and answered with a torrent of words that sounded half-hysterical. A dear little boy was lost, she cried. The poor child had been abandoned by his parents.

"There's the poor little mite, turned out of doors like a stray dog," the woman gulped, warming to her recital. "The kind of people in this world makes you sick! I suppose his father and mother didn't want to be bothered with him—though usually, I must say, they keep their boys. It's the girls who get left on doorsteps, but a child is a child and they never get over being rejected. Why, I know a case—"

Reade left her as she paused for breath and resumed his efforts to push his way through the mass, heedless of indignant retaliation. Dragging Leila and Holly, he finally gained the center of the crowd and came face to face with Robert.

Before Reade could speak, a patrolman struggled into view on the opposite side of the circle of spectators.

"What's the matter, sonny, you lost?" he asked the boy, ignoring the chorus of excited voices.

Robert, an ice cream cone in each hand and cake crumbs cascading down his coat, the pockets of which bulged with bags of peanuts and candy, sniffed tearfully. He did not look at Reade, but turned soulful brown eyes upon the Law.

"He left me," he wailed, as if heartbroken, but managed to lick up a gob of melting ice cream before he added, "All alone, by myself."

An indignant murmur ran through the crowd, and Reade stepped forward. "Cut it out, Robert," he commanded, more

76

savagely than he intended. "You'll be sick all night if you eat any more of that stuff," he warned automatically.

". . . pays no attention to a poor defenseless child," a high feminine voice babbled, as the crowd pressed closer.

Holly began to cry.

"You his father?" the patrolman demanded, eying Reade sternly.

"No, no, I'm not." Reade forced himself to speak calmly. "In fact, we're not related. He—"

". . . the little girl is scared to death of him—you can see it." A stout woman reached out to touch Holly, who immediately screamed. "Not used to kindness," the stout woman explained sadly.

The patrolman glanced from Robert, now eating one of his cones with placid enjoyment, to Reade, whose ruffled hair and perspiring face—he had given his handkerchief to Holly—did not inspire confidence.

"He says you're his father," the patrolman said. "You trying to get rid of the kid?"

"For God's sake!" Reade shouted. "Will you listen to me for a moment? I'm not his father. I'm his uncle. That is, not exactly his uncle—I'll have to explain."

Robert began to crunch the cone noisily. "Daddy?" he murmured experimentally.

A less sensitive man than Reade might have quailed at the look the patrolman gave him. Someone in the crowd offered help if "that bastard" resisted arrest. No one was prepared to have Leila place herself squarely before Robert and address him in a tone of withering scorn.

"Aren't you ashamed of yourself?" she cried angrily. "You got here all by yourself—we followed the popcorn. And Unkie is your *uncle*—at least, a make-believe uncle. I'm going to tell on you as soon as we get home, and I hope you get a spanking, so there!"

Inexplicably, this tirade had the desired effect. Robert visibly crumpled, and although he held fast to his remaining cone, he had lost interest in ice cream.

"People who tell lies go to hell," Leila remarked as a parting shot.

Reade, who thought he detected a developing inclination in her manner to address the curious crowd, suggested hastily that Robert must be tired and ready to go home. The patrolman still looked doubtful, but Reade's offer to give his name and address apparently made a favorable impression, and he escorted them to the gates and saw them into a taxi. His parting words to Reade, "I wouldn't want your job," indicated that he had listened attentively to the brief outline of Miss Mary's plan that Reade had thought it only fair to give him en route.

Reade himself was totally unprepared for the reaction of his charges as they spilled out of the taxi before the house and Jane came down to the curb to greet them.

"Have a good time?" she asked, smiling at the three beaming faces and trying not to catch Reade's eye.

"Unkie was so-o-o good," cooed Leila. "Thank you, dear." She stood on tiptoe and, as he bent down, kissed him.

Holly followed her example, and Robert, still clinging to the remnants of the ice cream cone, hurriedly wiped his free right hand on his coat before extending it. "Thank you very much, Unkie Reade," he said gravely.

6

"I suppose, in all fairness, it's just as hard on the rest of them as it is on me," Victoria May told her face in the mirror. "There are times when I wonder if I could have been in my right mind when I agreed to this insane arrangement."

She had been in the habit of talking to herself when she lived alone, and the pattern continued although now she was seldom without a listener. The years in which she had had her evenings to herself, those beautiful free hours to devote to work on her book, now seemed as unrealistic as a dream. As head of the typing pool in a large insurance firm, she had earned enough to support herself, in a rather narrow fixed routine, and to care for a retarded sister. Released from this responsibility by the sister's death, she had moved to a smaller apartment, and for the first time in the forty-seven years of her life she could follow her own desires. In that she had but one objective, she was fortunate—so many of the women she knew, imprisoned by real or fancied duties, dreamed of travel, of marriage, of careers possible only to the young. Victoria May belonged to that vast army of human souls who yearn "to write," a phrase that feebly expresses the scope of their dreams.

It had been the prospect of relief from the nagging restrictions of her budget that had induced her to join the family circle as outlined by Melinda Drew. In outline, at least, the plan had promised some free time, and some privacy, for everyone. What she had not had the brains to perceive (Victoria scowled at the face in the glass) was that odds and ends of free time offered her nothing. If, as sometimes happened, it took her an hour to write one sentence, what chance did she have of ever completing her book? The evenings to be spent in the living room might be envisioned as "cozy" by Miss Mary Hall, but for her they were sheer hell. And yet she intended to stick it out if it killed her. She had given her word.

At dinner that night Victoria found herself studying the twins. They had so much energy that surely some of it must be wasted. Would it be honorable to get them to take over part of her chores, leaving her, say, the afternoons free? She could afford to pay them, and they constantly announced that they were broke. Mrs. Hubbard might not care for the idea, and of course her consent would have to be obtained. But when she found herself alone in the kitchen with the twins' mother an hour later, Victoria, usually at no loss for words, was embarrassed.

"I hope you won't think I'm in favor of child labor," she blurted desperately. "But I did wonder—"

Elizabeth Hubbard, her attention divided between Victoria and the effort to decide how best to use up the leftover ham, said, "Yes, dear," and closed the refrigerator door. "An omelet, I think," she murmured. "You like omelets, don't you, Victoria?"

"I don't care," Victoria answered bitterly, "what I eat. All I ask is some time to myself. Do you think—would you be willing—after the twins get home from school in the afternoon, they could do a few things for me?"

Elizabeth, trying to remember who refused to eat eggs because of the cholesterol content, merely looked confused.

"Not that I want to get out of doing my fair share," Victoria said, with mounting emotion. "But lots of times they don't seem to have anything to do. I mean anything important."

"They're always doing their laundry," Mrs. Hubbard admitted. "And, of course, with all the equipment here, it's too much to expect them to keep out of the basement. But they are doing an excellent job of keeping the bathrooms clean and in order, don't you think?"

The bathrooms had been designated the responsibility of the twins, and for once, their father had been heard to say, they could slosh in water to their hearts' content.

"Well, never mind, I didn't really expect them to help me," Victoria sighed wearily. "But when I think of the lovely evenings I used to have, all to myself—"

She would perhaps be happier if she could knit or crochet, Elizabeth Hubbard said, not for the first time. She had confided to Grandma Lane that it drove her wild to watch Victoria "twiddling her thumbs" evening after evening. The two older men played checkers—chess they usually abandoned, finding it too difficult to concentrate in the articulate demonstrations of family life going on around them. Reade Coleman pretended to listen to the Spanish station on the radio—the twins were taking Spanish in their junior year of high school—and the twins themselves mysteriously managed to do their studying in the alcove of the living room.

The handsome, expensive television set had reluctantly

been supplied by Miss Mary, who had prophesied that it would destroy the atmosphere she was anxious to create. It was Melinda Drew's insistence that entertainment of some kind was necessary, if only to combat the lure of the movies, that had persuaded Miss Mary to change her mind. Neither she nor Melinda had foreseen the heated arguments, stopping just short of violence, that had resulted, sparked by the differences in tastes. No two persons could agree on any one program, and although Grandma Lane and Elizabeth (with years of experience and habit behind them) were willing to make concessions, the other members of the family defended their rights vociferously. The result was that the set was seldom used.

This evening Victoria was more restless than usual. Even the movies would be a relief, she thought, but she didn't like to go alone, and she certainly didn't feel like paying six dollars for two tickets. Ordinarily all movie fare bored her, but almost anything was better than wasting her time like this. Reade Coleman was fidgety, too, probably dying for a smoke: no one smoked in the living room, out of deference to Mr. Hubbard, whose doctor had advised him to give up tobacco.

The checkers players moved back their chairs, and Grandpa Lane's satisfied chuckle announced that he had won the set. His evening paper was awaiting him in a comfortable chair under a reading light, and Victoria realized with dismay that he was prepared to read it aloud. This distressing habit gave him such evident pleasure that no one had the heart to object openly. Indeed, Victoria suspected, half of his apparent listeners had trained themselves not to hear him at all. Unfortunately, she found it difficult to shut her mind to the sound of his monotonous voice.

"Care for a game?" Miles Hubbard's amused glance made her color with annoyance.

"I couldn't concentrate," she said coldly.

"The body of a young girl was found in an alleyway on East

Street," Grandpa Lane announced cheerfully. "Hasn't been identified. The chances these girls take! But they never learn."

The lack of comment failed to discourage him, and he read off the headlines slowly and carefully. A man had been murdered by his wife's lover, three children had been killed by the explosion of a stove, a rooming-house fire had made twenty old people homeless. In his dull but remarkably clear old voice, Grandpa Lane continued to read the day's ration of tragedy and crime. These presently exhausted, he turned to the editorials. Nor did he falter when he reached the women's page, although from the look his wife gave him she would have preferred to read that herself. Miles Hubbard and Reade were playing checkers now, and Victoria worked desperately on a crossword puzzle.

"Boil the avocado for fifteen minutes," the reader droned. "Next—"

"That's exactly like these newspaper recipes!" his wife interrupted indignantly. "You can't boil an avocado fifteen minutes. What would you have left?"

"It says fifteen minutes," Grandpa Lane insisted. "I guess whoever wrote the recipe knows how to make custard cups. Anyway, it says to boil the avocado."

Elizabeth Hubbard shook her head. "It's a misprint," she said firmly. "Half the time no one checks those recipes. And some poor bride with no experience wastes valuable time and expensive ingredients trying to follow the fool instructions."

Grandpa Lane had decided to skip the remaining recipes. Instead, he read a question-and-answer column in which the difficulties of keeping to a meatless diet, the problem of how large an allowance should be given to a child of four, and what to do when one's mother-in-law insisted on dropping in without advance notice were the topics discussed.

The twins, who seemed to have mastered the art of doing their homework and at the same time enjoying the evening's news, were interested in the question of an allowance for a four-year-old. No one had given him an allowance at that age, Ronnie complained, and Jane wanted to be told what a child could do with money at that age.

"It's another misprint," her mother assured her tolerantly. "When you were four years old you had your nickel every week for Sunday school and that was that. Really, proofreaders get more and more careless."

Grandpa Lane had now reached the financial page. Even he found that heavy going and willingly accepted Reade's suggestion that he skip the day's performance of stocks and substitute the columns on real estate. The weather report, saved to the last, as usual pleased no one, but the twins welcomed the possibility of light snow.

"I notice," said Grandma Lane in a slightly acid tone, as her husband carefully folded the paper—he never discarded a paper before it was two weeks old—"that you didn't read the advertisements. The department-store advertisements, I mean."

"A waste of good time," he assured her blandly.

"Well, I like to read the food-store prices," Elizabeth Hubbard said pleasantly. "Women have specific interests, you know. The price of lamb chops, for instance, could be more important than the stock-market news."

"What this house needs is another newspaper," Jane called from the alcove. "Get the *Evening Torch*, Mums. You'll love the women's page—the editor gave us a talk at school one day last winter."

Ronnie objected that the *Torch* was "lousy for sports," but conceded the *Globe* (from which Grandpa Lane had been reading) was not much better.

"I suppose we could take both papers—in the interests of peace," his father said slowly. "The radio commentaries apparently leave us unsatisfied."

A separate radio for each individual was the only solution they could see for the problem, he and Reade agreed later that evening. How it could happen that, in bringing together the members for her idealistic family circle, Miss Mary had managed to avoid finding at least *two* who thought alike was something he would never understand, Reade declared doggedly. Even the children seldom agreed on any point, and they bickered incessantly, although if an adult interfered they were loyal to each other.

"Well, there you have it," Miles Hubbard pointed out. "Three children, closely related, have differing opinions and tastes, and that's considered normal. Hell, my wife and I have our differences, too. Then why expect a group of virtual strangers, living an artificial—for it is artificial—existence, to be in accord? I'll just be thankful if we get through this business without any actual mayhem."

Two evenings later it was Reade who demanded to know why, with two papers delivered to the house, he should have to put up with tattered remnants when ready to read the copy he had brought home with him. To illustrate his complaint, he held up a page of the newspaper from which several items had been neatly clipped.

"Oh, I'm so sorry!" Grandma Lane apologized. "I saw the paper on the hall table, and I thought Caspar had brought it in. I only cut out the directions for dyeing a bedspread, and one other thing—I forget what it was. I left the clipping upstairs. I think—yes, I'm sure—it was about a new kind of diet."

She smiled gently at Reade, who could not forget that she had been responsible for serving his favorite pie twice that week. Let it be a lesson to him, he reflected gloomily, that nothing was safe in this house. He had had a dream the night before so vivid in detail that it had plagued him at intervals during the day.

In his dream he was one of a large group, all men, who slept in a dormitory, a long, narrow room, with a double row of beds facing each other. He knew that the beds were occupied, yet he had no distinct impression of any faces, nor did it seem to him that they were members of a religious order. The memory he retained most clearly was of the small white bags, one tied to each headboard. These bags, he knew, represented each man's sole personal possessions. He had nothing else to call his own. It was while he was trying to open his own bag, possessed by a sudden demoralizing certainty that it would be empty, that Reade had awakened. He had not been able to go back to sleep.

The twins were celebrating Friday night and release from homework by abandoning the alcove for the group in the living room. Their eagerness to discuss what they frankly called "the experiment" Victoria found rather terrifying. It made her feel, she told herself, like a fly stuck on a pin.

"I think what is needed," Jane remarked conversationally, watching her father and Reade set up the checkers board, "is better integration."

"Why don't we go in the alcove?" Reade suggested. "At least it's out of the mainstream."

"How did they manage in the good old days?" Ronnie put his question to Victoria in perfect friendliness and was unprepared for her glare.

She had no idea, she told him. As far as she was concerned, civilized people had always valued privacy. The depth of her feeling dismayed the boy, who hurriedly retreated to the corner where the three children—allowed to stay up an hour later on Friday—were putting a picture puzzle together.

"No, but there ought to be something that interests every one of us," Jane argued earnestly, shaking back her mane of hair. "I've been reading up on the—the past—and about taffy pulls and things like that. And dances—we could dance, I suppose?"

86

Not that she thought it made any sense to have a taffy pull when it was so much easier to make fudge, which tasted better, too. And she didn't see how the family could dance, unless they invited more people in who liked to waltz. In the dark ages, the—er—past, she meant to say, apparently the only dance had been the waltz.

Ronnie bounced to his feet, nearly knocking Leila over.

"Why don't we all go to the movies?" He radiated enthusiasm. "Not tonight, of course—it's too late—but tomorrow night. There's a great show at the Liberty. A spy story."

"It takes an argument to bring us all together," Miles Hubbard had cynically observed to Melinda Drew that afternoon, and now he was witnessing an illustration. The Lanes disliked spy stories, Reade Coleman labeled all screenplays "cheap," and Elizabeth Hubbard murmured that very few pictures were suitable for children to see.

But the children had heard the magic word "movies" and had rushed for the coat closet in the hall. Now they struggled back, weighted down by a miscellaneous collection of heavy coats and hats. Holly carried an umbrella.

"Ye gods, what next!" Reade dived forward to rescue his hat, tripped on the overcoat Robert was dragging, and went sprawling.

"We only wanted to help you get ready," Leila explained, with offended dignity, when order had been restored. "There's still time to go to the movies tonight if you hurry."

Elizabeth Hubbard, settling the question of movies for children at night, was extremely definite. The spy story sounded like a good matinee, she said, and Ronnie and Jane might take the children the next afternoon. The adults might wish to wait till the bill changed, but in any case they probably had no desire to be a part of the usual Saturday-afternoon audience.

"Almost any night next week we could all go," she suggested. "The twins will be studying and the children in bed.

There must be a good movie house somewhere in the neighborhood—the Liberty is a little too strong on Westerns and that type, don't you think?"

What to expect in the adult type of movie provided a discussion that continued after the children had been put to bed and Jane, who relieved her mother of this duty on most Friday nights, had returned to the living room. Ronnie was watching the checkers players, but Jane's whispered "How far have we got?" as she passed him elicited a clear response.

"Do you prefer the sex-saturated movie? Answer yes or no." Ronnie's glance did not swerve from the game board.

Victoria's needle jerked. "Well, *really*," she said.

"There's *The Trial Marriage* at the Bijou." Grandpa Lane's face was hidden by his newspaper. "And *The Shadow of Sin* is playing at the Majestic. I think that might be good."

"What I like is a good domestic comedy," his wife declared, paying no attention to the preference expressed. "Something that leaves a good taste in your mouth."

Jane glanced at her mother and made an expert diagnosis.

"Mums is dying for a little bridge," she informed the room. "Doesn't anyone want to play? I'm waiting for a phone call," she interpolated hastily, "so count me out."

Jane was an excellent bridge player, far better than Grandma Lane, whose conversational ability cards inevitably stimulated. It was hard on both twins, Elizabeth Hubbard thought, after the card table was set up, when Jane settled herself, with the sweater she was knitting for her brother, in a chair near the entrance to the hall. One telephone in a household the size of this was not enough—they all agreed to that. Almost daily the twins assured their mother that "almost all" of their contemporaries had individual phones, the expense in many instances paid for by the young subscriber from his or her own earnings. Not only was it difficult, indeed, practically impossible, for the twins to earn money, but Miss Mary's general indictment of the modern life style included specific criticism of the telephone. No one wrote letters any more; they telephoned. No one called on the bereaved; they telephoned condolences. Admittedly a convenience—although she deplored marketing by phone as one of the contributory causes of high prices—it should never have been allowed to substitute for the warmth of human contact. Jane, the dazed recipient of this homily, had tactfully reconsidered her earlier intention to mention the subject of boyfriends.

Ronnie left the checkers players and drifted around the bridge table. He paused beside his mother, looked at her hand, and gave her an encouraging pat on the shoulder, then strolled on toward Jane.

"It won't do you any good," he warned his sister. "The minute they hear the phone you'll have an attentive audience."

"Grandpa Lane is supposed to be deaf." Jane was derisive. "Bill thinks I ought to pretend I'm talking to a girl when he calls up, just to disappoint them. But I'm not cheating."

"Wait till you've got something to hide," Ronnie advised her. "But anyway, keep it brief. Tell Bill—" He broke off, and brother and sister jumped as the phone rang with that peculiar, shattering shriek that is its specialty.

In the living room, three of the bridge players turned startled faces toward the hall. Elizabeth Hubbard, who had been about to play a card, faltered. At the checkers table her husband unconsciously grunted, but Reade gave no sign of having heard anything.

"Yes, Bill, yes, it's me," Jane breathed into the phone, waved one hand wildly to her brother, who was producing an obviously counterfeit coughing spell. "Certainly I can hear you. Yes. I am all right—that isn't me coughing. Well, I can't shout. I told you how it would be. No. Well, there's nothing I can do about it—see you tomorrow. Good-bye."

"Don't blow your top!" Ronnie's whisper expressed his sympathy. "Fifty years from now you'll be married and all this will have been forgotten."

Jane laughed. She had told Bill Hazen not to call her, she said, but he hadn't believed her explanation of the built-in circle of listeners. He and his mother were newcomers to Acton, and Bill, transferring schools, had rapidly made friends with Jane, whose experience with the personal aspects of divorce had so far been mercifully limited.

"Bill's the product of a broken home," she had told her brother solemnly, making it sound, so Ronnie had told her, as if the victim had broken his leg.

Tonight, surveying the apparently placid scene in the living room, Jane found herself pondering whether the broken home might not present some definite advantages.

"Fifty years is an awfully long time to have to wait," she grumbled to Ronnie, and his assurance that it was always darkest just before the dawn failed to cheer her. "I'm probably wasting the best years of my life," she moaned. "Nothing ever changes here."

In that she was mistaken. For Victoria, making the beds a few mornings later, smoothly and now expertly and with incredible speed, was startled to have her routine interrupted. Anyone, she said later, justifying her sudden scream, would have been surprised to find a strange dog in the center of Reade Coleman's bed.

The dog was large, shaggy, very dirty, and not at all pleased to be asked to move. Victoria threw a pillow at him, with no effect. When she threatened him with a broom, hastily snatched from the broom closet, he growled unpleasantly.

"Well, I'm not going to argue with you, no matter what you think!" Victoria informed him. "As far as I'm concerned you can stay there the rest of the day."

She closed the bedroom door sharply and ran hurriedly

down to the dining room. Only Grandma Lane and Elizabeth Hubbard remained at the breakfast table. To her flustered "Where's everybody?" they answered that Grandpa Lane was off on his morning walk, the other two men had left for their offices, and the twins had gone to school, dropping the three children at *their* school on the way.

"We thought you were dressing to go out, dear," Grandma Lane said. "Is anything the matter? I have the grocery list ready for you."

"Nothing's the matter." Victoria spoke grimly. "Except that there's a perfectly enormous, perfectly filthy dog in the middle of Reade Coleman's bed, and I can't budge him."

7

Grandma Lane said, "Oh dear!" and Elizabeth's face reflected
the apprehension of mothers who hope they are prepared to
hear the worst.

"I don't see how a dog could get there," she said anxiously.
"The twins didn't leave the house last night, and they never
went out this morning until they were ready for school."

Victoria nodded acceptance of the cup of coffee Grandma
Lane handed her, but declined to sit down. She didn't blame
the twins; it must be Reade Coleman's idea of a joke. (Some
people had a perverted sense of humor.) The question was,
what should be done about the dog?

"No one but a man would leave for the office without telling you," she said. "For all I know he may be vicious. No one

but a man would leave a strange dog on his bed and go off without saying a word."

Grandma Lane suggested charitably that the dog might be as great a surprise to Reade as to Victoria, but she spoke without much conviction. And when Elizabeth Hubbard phoned Reade at his office an hour later, he readily assumed responsibility. The dog had followed him home the night before, he said, and was evidently a stray.

"You can see he's been abused. The poor fellow was so grateful for a few kind words that I couldn't get rid of him when we reached the house. He's part collie and part retriever, I think."

How had the dog got into the house without being seen? He had left him outside until after the household quieted down for the night, Reade explained. He had thought the dog might have left by that time.

"But no, there he was when I opened the door. And so damn glad to see a friendly face, how could I leave him? I brought him upstairs with me, and he never stirred all night— just exhausted. He'll be all right till I get home. Of course, he needs a bath—"

It was pointed out to him that he couldn't expect a dog to stay shut up all day in a room without food or water. And if he, Reade, did not care whether his bed was made or not, it was unthinkable to leave the dog in possession until his new master came home for dinner.

"It's simply impossible for me to leave now." Reade glared at the handiest object, which happened to be his secretary, with pencil poised above her notebook. "What about the twins?"

"What about them?" the twins' mother demanded coldly.

They could do something about the dog, Ronnie especially. Boys liked dogs; in fact, he had heard Ronnie wish several times that he had a dog. The twins would be home from school early in the afternoon, and they could handle Wednesday.

"Handle *who?*" Elizabeth Hubbard motioned Grandpa Lane to stand back from the phone—he had returned from his walk and was evidently trying to catch up on such conversation as he had missed.

Wednesday was the dog's name, Reade asserted in desperation. There wasn't the slightest chance that the dog would bite anyone, Ronnie least of all. Well, suppose the poor animal *had* growled at the broom. A dog with any intelligence would object to a female—er—a woman—poking at him with a broom.

"I'll try to get home an hour earlier," he fibbed rapidly. "That's the best I can do. You don't need to call the police— Ronnie will know what to do."

Elizabeth Hubbard, replacing the phone, was momentarily stunned.

"He says the dog's name is Wednesday," she said to the two old people, who stared at her curiously. "Sometimes I think I must be going mad!"

It would be better, they all agreed, to say nothing to the children, whose school day ended with the morning session. One of the neighboring mothers picked them up at noon with her own youngsters and delivered them with the cheerful air of one leaving valuable small packages. After lunch, Leila and Holly had their naps while Robert amused himself after his own fashion—at times, Miles Hubbard suspected, he suffered from too much feminine companionship.

The dog was not mentioned until the twins reached home a little after two o'clock. Despite a substantial lunch, they were in their usual state of starvation and intent upon raiding the refrigerator. With Robert at their heels, they made sandwiches and set out the milk, and were ready to refresh their exhausted frames, when to their astonishment their mother, followed by Grandpa and Grandma Lane, filed into the kitchen.

"I have something to tell you," Elizabeth Hubbard said, unconscious that her voice suggested a disaster.

Jane, always sensitive to the slightest nuance, was instantly alarmed.

"What happened? Don't you feel well, Mother? Is Daddy—"

"Good gracious, child, nothing's the matter," Grandma Lane assured her briskly. "That is, nothing very serious. And your mother's all right."

Ronnie patted his mother's shoulder, his invariable caress.

"My conscience's clear, Mums," he encouraged her. "Anything you hear to the contrary just isn't so."

"Well, let your mother finish what she was going to say," Grandpa Lane said a little irritably. "There's so much talk in this house it's a wonder anyone ever listens. Speak out, Elizabeth. You were saying—"

She glanced toward him gratefully. "What I started to say is that there's a dog—he belongs to Reade Coleman—in the house."

For a startled moment no one spoke. Then Ronnie, whose mouth had been full, managed to swallow a large bite of sandwich roll.

"A dog? Where? *Whose* dog? Why didn't you tell us, Mums?" He stopped short as a sharp bark sounded from the upstairs region.

"No, wait—let me tell you." His mother's effort to speak calmly was a failure. "It's on Reade Coleman's bed and I can't get him off. When I tried, he growled at me."

Jane stared at her mother in astonishment, but Ronnie began to laugh.

"Oh, boy! On Reade's *bed!* I can see the fireworks when he

gets home tonight, even if it is his dog. Don't do anything to spoil it, Mums!"

"Don't be silly," Jane adjured him, instantly taking the housewife's view. "Mums wants to make the bed—golly, where was Vicky? How come she didn't see the dog?"

Victoria had seen the dog, her mother said patiently, but had not been able to dislodge it. No, the dog had had nothing to eat, and she shuddered to think of the condition the room must be in by now.

"We'll clean it up," Ronnie promised, with heart-warming enthusiasm. "Come on, Jane, to the rescue!"

His mother and Grandma Lane followed them to the foot of the stairs, and Grandpa Lane kept a firm grip on Robert.

"Try not to wake the children," Grandma Lane implored, and Elizabeth Hubbard called helpfully that Reade had said the dog's name was Wednesday.

Ronnie opened the bedroom door and staggered back from the impact of a tawny, shaggy body that hurled itself upon him with every evidence of affection. Wednesday's tail wagged frantically as he tried to lick the boy's face and hands, clearly accepting Ronnie as a long-lost friend. Dirty he might be, and he was far from odorless, but there was no mistaking his sincerity.

Jane had slipped past him and stood surveying the bed with extreme distaste. Unkie, she predicted, would have a fit. "But the poor dog couldn't help it. Why don't you take him down to the cellar, Ronnie, and feed him? He must be starved. I can clean up this mess."

Wednesday needed a bath almost as much as he needed food, Ronnie declared, and if the kids would keep out of the way he could manage to supply both. Leila and Holly, wakened by the commotion, had joyfully scuttled out in their bathrobes and were gazing in mixed horror and fascination at the bewildered animal. Leila was sure it was a lion, but her first thought, that it might have eaten Robert, was discarded when she glimpsed him standing in the hall below.

"I'll come help you," Jane called cheerfully as she wrestled with the bed linen. "He'll be nice-looking, once he's cleaned up."

Ronnie and the dog, trailed by the three children—Robert had been released, with an admonition to look after his sisters—disappeared into the cellar depths. Jane, bundling together the soiled sheets from Reade's bed, looked up to see her mother in the doorway.

"You didn't have to do this, dear," Mrs. Hubbard said, watching half enviously the beautiful, superbly effortless movements of the slim young body. "I don't know what we're to do about that dog," she added.

Jane, unfolding a fresh sheet, looked astonished.

"You mean Wednesday? Why, if he's Unkie's dog, I think it's very sweet of him to want to keep him. Somehow I never thought of Unkie being the type to care about dogs."

Automatically Elizabeth Hubbard began to help with the bedmaking, but her mind still wrestled with the dog problem.

"I simply don't see how we can have a dog," she worried. "It's all right for Reade—he isn't here during the day. Dogs have to be taken out, and we certainly can't expect Grandpa Lane to do that. Think of the trouble it will mean in bad weather."

Wednesday would be no trouble at all, her daughter assured her. Let Unkie Reade walk him early in the morning and the last thing at night.

"Ronnie or I will take him out when we get home from school—of course he has to have a license and a collar and leash."

Everything would turn out all right, Jane prophesied, assuming the increasingly familiar role of comforter. Older people, she thought resignedly, had such a dreary way of always looking on the dark side.

"You've often said that a good watchdog is better than burglar alarms, Mums. Well, now you've got yourself a good watchdog."

Wednesday, bountifully fed, thoroughly washed and dried, presented a more trustworthy appearance, Elizabeth Hubbard conceded. She advanced the money for a collar and leash, but said firmly that the matter of a license was Reade's responsibility. Nor would she allow the twins to walk the dog farther than the length of the block before he was properly tagged. No child of hers, she told them, was going to have a record of arrest, especially when the dog didn't even belong to them.

"They don't arrest you—you only get a summons," Ronnie protested. "And half the dogs you see out every night haven't a license, anyway."

However, Reade proved surprisingly appreciative of what Jane rather confusedly referred to as the "postnatal care" bestowed upon his ungainly possession. Over the protests of both parents, he insisted that the dog-walking chore must be placed upon a businesslike basis. It was only fair, he said, since inevitably the duty must at times conflict with the twins' other commitments. The arrangement delighted the twins, who solemnly assured him that at least one of them would always be at Wednesday's service.

Unfortunately, the dog's improved outward appearance did not extend to his personal habits, notably his fondness for sleeping on beds. Aside from the kitchen, where he was unwelcome, the bedrooms seemed to be the only places that attracted him. In vain, Grandma Lane constructed inviting rug-lined corners for his repose. He would have none of them. Neither could he be induced to nap on the living-room couch—Elizabeth Hubbard's concession to his evident dislike of floor level. He remained determined to sleep on beds, and could be circumvented only by everybody's keeping the bedroom doors closed—a practice, Grandma Lane complained, that made her feel as if she were living in a hotel. But he endeared himself to Grandpa Lane by his habit of sitting close beside him in the evening, his head on the old man's knee. Both dozed fitfully, and if the newspaper slipped to the floor Wednesday tried politely to pick it up.

"I'm a little tired of being snubbed by that dog," Grandma Lane confided one morning, as she and Elizabeth were enjoying their second cup of coffee in the peaceful solitude of the deserted breakfast table. "The only time he knows I'm around is when he wants to be fed."

Both women glanced coldly at Wednesday, who lay sprawled comfortably between the kitchen and dining room.

"He can't compare with a nice cat," Grandma Lane said, and at the magic word the sensitive silky ears stood up.

Elizabeth Hubbard buttered a strip of coffee cake. "I don't know why we shouldn't have a cat, do you?" she asked.

Grandma Lane's eyes, behind her spectacles, sparkled with delight. "We always had a cat when I kept house," she recalled. "Mostly they were Maltese. Where are you going?" She broke off suddenly, as her companion hastily stood up.

The supermarket cat had had another litter of kittens, Elizabeth informed her. "She had only two left when I was there yesterday—her kittens are famous, and the manager never has any trouble finding homes for them. I'd better catch the next bus. I hate to leave you with the dishes—" But she was already in the hall, struggling into her coat and tying a kerchief over her gray hair. Watching her, Grandma Lane saw for a moment a reflection of Jane's youthful vigor.

In less than an hour she was back, carrying a stout paper bag from which she spilled out a tiny black kitten.

"Not a white hair on him. Isn't he lovely?" Elizabeth

reached down to pick up the kitten, but Wednesday had already seen it.

The two women watched him as he carefully sniffed the ball of black fur, from which faint hisses issued and an infinitesimal paw shot out to land on his nose. Wednesday merely continued to wag his tail, his expression benign.

"He'll be good to it," Elizabeth said with relief. "As a rule dogs take kindly to kittens—even full-grown dogs, I mean. It's the cats who never trust them."

Grandma Lane, who had been mentally arranging an empty shoe box to serve as the newcomer's bed, wondered about a suitable name. "For pity's sake, don't let's call him Inky," she begged. "I must have known a hundred black cats, all named Inky."

In her relief that she had not suggested the obvious, although she had been on the point of doing so, Elizabeth Hubbard clutched gratefully at a fleeting idea. Why not, she said, leave the choice of a name to a popular vote?

"Tonight, when everyone's home, we can let them decide," she urged. "It will give them the feeling of sharing the kitten— even if no two of them can agree on the right name," she finished, joining in Grandma Lane's gentle laughter.

The twins expressed a tolerant interest in the kitten, and the three children were delighted and took it upon themselves to break the news to Victoria as soon as she entered the house. She had been at an all-day session of the Women's Club.

"We've got a cat!" they screamed in unison. "A lovely black cat. Black cats are lucky—did you know that? Come and see our lovely kitty."

Victoria, sidestepping Wednesday's welcome, peered suspiciously around her feet. Wasn't a dog enough trouble, she demanded? Whose idea was it to add a cat?

"It's a kind of finishing touch, don't you think?" Grandma Lane, murmuring endearments, scooped up the kitten from the floor. She hoped it would lap warm milk, she said, but if not she could feed it with a medicine dropper.

The kitten provided the chief topic of conversation at the dinner table that night, and competition for naming it proved unexpectedly vigorous. Miles Hubbard finally suggested that they hold a drawing, each contestant to write his choice for a name on a slip of paper. By common consent, the dining-room table was left uncleared while Ronnie cut a sheet of paper into slips and his mother produced an empty brass bowl. Everyone, she insisted, must be allowed a "vote," and, yes, she would write the slips for Leila and Holly. Their choices of names, whispered sibilantly in her ear, were Inky and Blackie. Ronnie passed the bowl around and, all the slips deposited, stirred the contents thoroughly with a letter opener.

"Let Holly make the drawing," Jane suggested. "I'll blindfold her, and she's allowed one grab."

Holly was delighted with her role, and it was decided that Grandpa Lane should hold the bowl. Blindfolded, Holly was gently guided toward him, and plunged a little fat hand into the bowl.

"Just one!" Jane admonished. "Just one slip, dear. Drop the rest—that's right. Now stand still—a minute—there you are!"

Victoria was heard to mutter something about "a feeble-minded performance," but she pressed forward as eagerly as the others.

Jane, having extracted the slip from Holly's possessive small fingers, handed it solemnly to her father.

"Looks like the kitten's name is going to be Midnight," he announced.

Grandpa Lane bounced in his chair so excitedly that he almost dropped the bowl. "That's my name!" he crowed. "Midnight. Yes sir, had a kitten named that when I was a boy in grade school."

"Well, I think Topaz would have been prettier," his wife said. "The kitten's eyes are a topaz color."

Victoria May disagreed. When she had noticed the creature's eyes they had been distinctly green. "And I still think Esmeralda would be more appropriate."

"Is it a she?" inquired Ronnie with interest.

Victoria retorted crossly that she didn't know and didn't care—a euphonious name was her only concern.

Reade Coleman had already retired with his evening paper to his favorite—and the best—spot under a reading lamp. Appealed to by Jane for his opinion, he said he thought Midnight rather banal and refused to reveal the name he had written on his slip.

"Poor Wednesday," Jane crooned, patting the dog, who had managed to look both offended and dignified during the proceedings and now manifested the liveliest interest in the contents of the bowl. "There's nothing to eat in that. Come on out to the kitchen and I'll give you dinner."

Ronnie offered to empty the brass bowl, and followed his sister into the kitchen. Would she, he asked in a conspiratorial whisper, recognize Unkie's handwriting? Jane thought she would. Ronnie had just time enough to stuff the slips into his pocket before his mother looked in on them to ask the familiar question of whether they had any studying to do that night.

Half an hour later the two students, ostensibly tackling the problems of homework in the semiprivacy of the alcove, appeared at intervals to be overcome by mirth. Ronnie suffered several coughing fits, and his sister mopped her eyes and blew her pretty nose. Neither of them, they assured their concerned mother, thought they had taken cold.

They had sorted the slips of paper saved from the brass bowl, and Jane had identified the name Superfluous as Reade's contribution. She was positive of the identification—no one, she insisted, could duplicate his letter S.

"Besides, I ask you, who else would want to give a poor little innocent cat a name like that? I hope," said Jane, her indignation mounting, "that when Midnight grows up he will scratch him."

But Midnight—in less than a week his name was shortened by universal consent to Middy—settled down into the household placidly and betrayed no animosity. Wednesday, quick to recover from a mild attack of jealousy, soon became so attached (literally) to the small ball of fur that they were seldom apart. The dog endured the kitten's antics with the patient tolerance of an elderly friend, allowed Middy to ride on his back, swing from the end of his long hair, and sleep between his paws. The twins declared that he deliberately shortened his daily walks, and certainly on his return he faithfully searched the house for his small friend.

Unfortunately, Wednesday's fondness for beds remained an indelible characteristic. The necessity for keeping the bedroom doors closed continued to irritate the womenfolk, but nothing, the men said, could be done about it. Wednesday was too old a dog to be trained, and the alternative of giving him up was too painful even to be discussed. The children, not to mention the twins, would be brokenhearted, and even the adults admitted that, as Grandma Lane said, he filled a niche and his absence would be felt.

"That can be taken in two ways," she had told the confused twins.

But the fate of Wednesday became extremely precarious when, the next week, he and the kitten were discovered asleep in the center of Victoria May's bed. She had come back to pick up a forgotten shopping list and had neglected to close the door of her room as she left. Her nerves, rasped by a disappointing search for bargains, were completely frayed by the sight of the complacent pair sprawled luxuriously on her immaculate bedspread when she returned to her room at dinnertime.

"Of all the unspeakable, dirty, outrageous animals!" she screamed, tossing her heavy shoulder bag at the startled offenders. "Get out of here! Do you hear me? Get out of here!"

The dog and the kitten leaped from the bed, collided violently with the rescuers crowding the doorway, and escaped down the stairs.

"Well, I do think, Elizabeth," Grandma Lane observed, when peace had been restored and dinner served and eaten, "that she made a little too much fuss. If Wednesday had been a mad dog, frothing at the mouth, she couldn't have screamed any louder."

But it was Grandma herself who aroused the household with a piercing shriek a few days later. It was a Saturday morning and her turn to do the marketing. She was humming contentedly as she opened a bureau drawer to get a fresh handkerchief. Something small and black darted out and dashed madly across the rug, to sit huddled in a corner.

"What happened?" Miles Hubbard had been halfway up the stairs and was the first to reach her.

"Are you hurt? Did you scream?" Victoria opened her bedroom door and called.

Grandma Lane looked apologetically at the group of worried faces and tried to smile. "It was the kitten—Middy," she explained. "He was in the bureau drawer. He kind of startled me."

Jane had already found the frightened little cat and was cuddling it in her hands. "You scared him," she said.

"Well, he scared me," Grandma Lane retorted. "He must have been in that drawer all night. My nice handkerchiefs are all stirred up—he used them for a bed."

Reade Coleman—he had been in the cellar when he heard

the commotion—muttered that cats were the very devil. "If they're not under your feet they are scrambling around in places they've no business to be. A dog at least has a little sense."

Grandma Lane said shakily that she had been startled. It was not the fault of Middy. Cats always liked dark, enclosed places, she said; it was natural for them to like to hide.

"When we had a cat at home she always had her kittens in the last place you'd think to look for them," she finished triumphantly.

The expression on Reade's face was matched by that on Victoria's, but he spoke first.

"You don't mean to tell me that cat is going to have kittens!" His tone of utter horror sent Jane reeling against Ronnie, whose suppressed laughter was already strangling him.

"For pity's sake!" Elizabeth Hubbard might have been speaking to Holly. "The poor little thing isn't more than two months old. And now, if Grandma Lane is all right, why don't we get on with the morning jobs? Where's Robert? The children haven't taken their vitamins yet."

Ronnie looked oddly at Jane, who still seemed to be suffering from the giggles. But she suddenly gave a loud hiccup and announced herself to be all right.

"Come on." Her brother jerked his head toward the stairs. "I know where Robert is."

Jane followed him meekly up to the third floor and into what would have been the trunk room, had, as Victoria once tartly observed, anyone possessed a trunk. She had rather bitterly criticized the modern preference for suitcases and carry-alls, and had aroused the curiosity of Robert, who had taken to haunting the trunk room, possibly in hope of one day finding a trunk.

Robert, standing in the center of the room, glared at them defiantly. The morning sun streamed in through a dormer window but revealed no trace of dust. A few boxes, neatly tied up, and a couple of badly scuffed leather suitcases were stowed against one wall. There was nothing else in the room.

The background was familiar enough to Jane, but Robert, facing them and scowling, filled her with dismay. He was dressed as he had been at breakfast, but in his right hand he held—Jane caught her breath and for a paralyzing moment shut her eyes—he held a revolver.

"Is—is that real?" Jane gulped.

"You bet it's real," said Ronnie's voice, behind her. "What's more, the damn thing is loaded. He let me take a look at it. I was afraid he might shoot himself before I could get you up here."

Robert nonchalantly rested the muzzle of his weapon on the floor. The weight of the revolver evidently was too much for him. He looked at Jane and the scowl relaxed.

"It's mine," he told her. "I found it and it's mine. I won't let old Ronnie have it."

Behind her Ronnie urged, "Ask him where he found it. And whose gun it is."

"Don't you two communicate?" an irritated Jane demanded. "Where did you find the gun, Robert?"

"Outdoors," he said briefly. "I didn't want the girls to get it."

By "the girls" he meant his sisters, and Jane in her relief could have kissed him. But there was still the loaded revolver to be disposed of. And there should be an owner of the thing somewhere.

"Whose gun is it?" she questioned, and even to her the words sounded foolish.

Robert didn't know whose gun he had found. It had been "in the bushes." Wednesday, digging there, had attracted his attention.

Jane's excited voice had carried, and the adults had climbed the stairs to peer into the room over her shoulder.

"The thing must belong to someone," Grandma Lane fretted. "Suppose he comes back to get it?"

For some reason this sounded funny to Jane, and she laughed, rather hysterically. "He'll have to ring the bell and ask for his revolver," she giggled. "Perhaps he'll offer a reward."

"Don't be silly," admonished her father. "Robert, let me have that revolver—now, this minute."

Robert looked at him and decided to obey. He handed the weapon, muzzle end first, to Miles and burst into tears.

"It's mine. I found it!" he sobbed. "Why can't I keep it?"

He was soothed by the assurance that he could be the one to tell the policeman about his find, although when a very tall, quiet-spoken officer appeared in answer to a phone call Robert was suddenly stricken mute and had to be coaxed to answer the questions asked.

Why a loaded revolver should have been tucked away in a bush in the front yard of a private home puzzled the police as much as it did the household. Indeed, the officer, listening to a brief explanation of Miss Mary's experiment, found that arrangement even more mystifying. No one, he reported to his partner in the prowl car, was related to anyone else, except the three children to each other, and the Hubbards, who were the parents of the twins.

"If I lived in a family like that I'd keep a revolver handy so I could shoot myself before I went crazy," the partner commented.

And for the next fifteen minutes they seriously debated the question whether it was more "sensible" to commit suicide outside a house than within, and where, with that end in view, would be the handiest place to stow a loaded revolver.

They left behind them an atmosphere not precisely reassuring.

"They said they'll keep an eye on the house for the next few weeks," Elizabeth Hubbard remarked. "What do you suppose that means?"

"Oh, I think they expect the owner of the revolver to come back for it," her husband answered matter-of-factly. "Not that he'll ring the bell and *ask* for it, Libby. He'll just sneak around, and they hope they can catch him you might say unawares."

"Lock the first-floor windows every night," Ronnie advised his apprehensive mother.

"Can I sit up and watch for him?" Robert said.

8

No one came back for the revolver, and after a week or two the incident had been almost forgotten except by Grandma Lane, and by Robert, who coveted the weapon to bolster the tales he told in school. Grandma, a poor sleeper at best, began to hear strange "noises" at night, which she confusedly identified with a mysterious stranger's search for his lost revolver. If she and Robert could have brought themselves to compare notes, each of them would have been assured a sympathetic listener.

After the usual number of false starts, the spring finally decided on an early debut. Grandpa Lane, who had been restrained with difficulty throughout March, could now watch the earth for his garden being turned by two strong young men. They found his enthusiasm for gardening mildly amusing, and predicted that when the time came for weeding he would be glad to get his vegetables from the supermarket. All vegetables were planted and weeded and picked by machinery these days, they told him. And they hinted that in the machine age no one in his right mind dreamed of trying to grow *food*.

Reade Coleman, who, with Miles Hubbard, was fitting the new full-length screens over the windows on a Saturday morning, had overheard the desultory argument. When the men had shouldered their spades and left, he and the old man exchanged grins. For a moment they both watched the retreating backs of the workers, noting half enviously their free, swinging stride.

"Have to be young to do it." Grandpa Lane sighed. "Half an hour of digging like that and I couldn't move, come tomorrow."

"Well, I think I'd be a little stiff myself," Reade conceded. "You use muscles you don't ordinarily call on. Think you can do the rest of it yourself?"

He might cheat a little if he could get Ronnie to help him, the old man said. But aside from stooping he didn't anticipate much trouble.

He was certainly using some muscles himself that he had forgotten he possessed, Reade acknowledged to Miles Hubbard as they wrestled with the screens. They had been built to measure for every window in the house, and represented not only a considerable outlay of cash but also a compromise on the part of Miss Mary. She was violently opposed to air conditioning, believing it had caused the deaths of two of her friends. Nothing would induce her to have air conditioning in her own home, and nothing could persuade her to have it installed under any conditions for which she considered herself responsible. Good screens kept out flies and did not interfere with the currents of fresh air, she preached—and practiced.

"We may be thankful for the screens if the save-a-watt campaign continues through the summer," Reade admitted to his colleague. "But if ever I build a house—God forbid!—it won't have so many windows."

The children had been fascinated by the spading, and now they followed Grandpa Lane up and down the length of the spaded strip, stopping when he stopped and almost falling over him in their eagerness to learn how a garden was made. Wednesday followed happily in their rear, doubtless recalling past gardening efforts that had resulted in turning up delicious, smelly old bones.

"Now look here!" Grandpa, short of breath but exuding contentment, seated himself on the back-porch steps. "I don't know what you young ones think is going to happen, but don't look for anything to be growing yet. I haven't planted any seeds—you have to be patient."

Robert, who had lingered at the far end of the deep lot, came galloping toward them, holding something in his hand.

"I didn't eat it," he exclaimed virtuously.

All the children had given their solemn word not to taste or eat anything they might find without first showing it to an adult.

"It's rhubarb." Grandpa Lane identified the limp green stalk.

"It's good to eat," he assured the boy. "A little on the sour side, maybe. My mother wouldn't think it was spring unless we had stewed rhubarb. Makes good pie, too. Where did you find it, Bobby?"

The other two children were immediately interested and eager to see the rhubarb plant. Robert, with all the importance of a trained guide, led them to the end of the lot and pointed out the shoots bursting through the brown earth. When, Leila asked, had the rhubarb been planted, and Holly wanted to know who had planted it. And when they understood that it had probably been coming up year after year, without special attention, Robert suggested that perhaps it had been a mistake to "dig up" earth for a garden. Why not, he said, just let everything grow as the rhubarb did?

But he listened politely to the old man's explanation, while the two little girls and the dog raced back to the house. After all, he, Robert, held the evidence in his own right hand, and although the girls might make the announcement, he would be the one to display the exciting proof.

"Grandma says she'll make us a rhubarb pie!" Leila was dancing about the back porch when they reached the steps.

"Maybe it isn't rhubarb." Holly was evidently prepared to mourn. Her lips quivered; her lovely eyes expressed deep sympathy.

Robert mounted the steps, the squashed stalk dangling from his fingers, Grandpa Lane behind him. Now, their attitude proclaimed, was the time for men to stand together.

Grandma Lane met them at the door, and Robert placed the shreds in her outstretched hand.

"Why, of course it's rhubarb. How lovely!" She smiled. "I'll wash it off and you can eat it, if you like."

With Leila and Holly watching, Robert took a tentative bite.

"Sour!" he said explosively. And added, "You can have the pie."

In spite of all explanations and cautions, the children could not fully accept the repeated assurances that a garden required time to grow. It wasn't like instant coffee, Ronnie was overheard telling them—you could not drop a seed into the earth, pour on a little water, and have peas or beans or tomatoes leap out.

"A gardener," Ronnie instructed his disappointed audience, "has to have lots of patience."

As he might have expected, Jane told him, this involved

him in explanations of why the rhubarb, which had not been planted at all, should grow so quickly and abundantly.

"Never explain," Jane counseled her twin. "You only get bogged down. My method is to distract their attention."

"A fine teacher you're going to make," her mother, overhearing this advice, commented. "I thought a cardinal rule of child psychology was to answer every question."

The budding spring was presenting Elizabeth Hubbard, and Grandma Lane as well, with a variety of problems more or less personal. Both women were made secretly uneasy by the realization that in a house where everything was new and freshly installed there was no need for the traditional spring cleaning. The satisfaction of "turning a room inside out," creating chaos and uprooting cherished debris, was an annual event to which they looked forward, although neither would have admitted it. Where everything was already fresh and clean, there was no disorder to be restored, and they were restless.

Their situation, while not clearly understood by the other members of the family, was vaguely realized. They were advised by Grandpa Lane to "get out in the air." Miles Hubbard suggested to his wife that perhaps she should see the doctor for a checkup. And the twins enthusiastically recommended "a long walk in the woods."

"You stay in the house too much, Mums," Ronnie said, making himself an enormous sandwich as an after-school snack. "You'll get a better appetite if you take a good long tramp."

Probably in desperation, certainly without pleasant expectations, his mother promised that she and Grandma Lane would take a walk in the woods the next day. For all they knew, the place might be full of tramps, Grandma Lane suggested dismally, but she supposed that if attacked they could scream loudly enough to frighten anyone off.

"I read in the paper that a woman's best weapon, if she is attacked, is to scream at the top of her voice," she said at the dinner table.

Jane choked. "For heaven's sake, Gram, this is supposed to be a walk for pleasure," she gulped. "The woods are safe. And anyway, there isn't enough foliage yet to hide anyone. Take Wednesday—he'll love it."

The twins, detained by a late class meeting, raced home the next afternoon—not, they carefully explained to Grandpa Lane, working in his garden, to check on the seekers after fresh air, but merely to hear how much they had enjoyed the walk.

"They could walk a little farther every day," Jane planned cheerfully, "and in no time at all they could be doing two miles at a stretch."

Grandpa Lane, busy with tape measure and twine, considered this optimistic program gravely.

"I don't think it's very likely that they'll ever be walking two miles a day," he said. "Matter of fact, I doubt if you ever get them to set foot in those woods again."

The twins glanced toward the house.

"Nothing to worry about," the old man assured them. "I think your mother and Grandma are lying down. Said they didn't need the doctor."

"The doctor!" Ronnie and Jane chorused. "What happened?"

Jane raced up the front steps, Ronnie at her heels. They burst into the house, to be confronted by their startled mother.

"Are you hurt?" she demanded anxiously. "What happened?"

Behind her, Grandma Lane, a long-handled mixing spoon in her hand, echoed the questions.

"We're all right," Ronnie assured them impatiently. "But what about you? Grandpa said something about you lying down."

"Just like him!" Grandma Lane spoke crossly. "We might

have dropped down for a minute or two, just to catch our breath. But with dinner to see to, what would be the sense of staying in bed?"

Jane's eyes met her mother's.

"I suppose it will sound very silly to you," Elizabeth Hubbard admitted. "But the truth is we had a shock."

"Oh, darling!" Jane's commiseration was instant. "Did you meet a tramp? I thought Wednesday would always protect you."

"Did you faint, Mums?" Ronnie inquired with interest.

She had never fainted in her life and didn't intend to begin now, his mother informed him.

"And don't talk to me about a dog being a protection. Wednesday never even saw it until Grandma Lane screamed."

Anyone would have screamed, Grandma Lane assured the twins defensively. She wasn't any more nervous than the average woman, but the sudden fright had upset her.

"*What* frightened you?" Jane restrained an impulse to add, "If anything."

"If you must know," her mother replied with dignity, "it was a snake."

A horror-stricken Jane repeated blankly, "A snake?" and immediately pictures of boa constrictors and other deadly reptiles she had seen at the zoo flashed through her mind.

Ronnie was also shaken, but managed to ask if the snake had been alive. For some reason this query affronted his mother.

"Of course it was alive!" She shuddered. "A great, ugly, writhing thing that slithered directly across our path. That's the last time I ever set foot in those ghastly woods."

Grandma Lane nodded in confirmation. No, she didn't know what kind of a snake it was, and she didn't care. What difference did it make even if, as Ronnie kept interrupting her to say, it was only a harmless snake awaking from its winter

115

hibernation? A snake was a snake—people weren't meant to like them. Anyone who read his Bible would know what she meant.

"I'll bet that finishes the walks in the woods," Ronnie said to Jane. "By tomorrow that snake will be a deadly asp. Or do I mean adder?"

"Both are easy to spell," Jane reminded him kindly. "That's probably the reason you remember them. Anyway, it's too bad that Mums should see any kind of snake on her first walk. She's cooped up in the house too much, and so is Grandma Lane. I wish she—or they—really liked to play bridge."

Ronnie, puzzled, asked what exercise could be derived from playing bridge, and was told that the bridge table was an ideal place for the exchange of ideas.

"For instance, one woman might remark that she had to walk every day, doctor's orders, and that she always brought home some kind of a souvenir. Something she found or picked up, something that cost her nothing. That would give Mums an incentive to vary her walks, and, who knows, in time she might find she had a remarkable collection."

Ronnie observed that "remarkable" would undoubtedly be the correct descriptive adjective. After a moment of silence, Jane suggested tactfully that men seemed to find it easier to dispose of their leisure time than women did. Grandpa Lane, for instance, could always entertain himself by taking the bus into town. Women, Jane thought, usually felt a little guilty if they tried to enjoy themselves alone.

"You remember Mother when we were young." Jane spoke with perfect seriousness. "She almost never went anywhere without taking one or both of us along. It gets to be a habit, I think. Now that she has freedom, she doesn't know how to use it, poor love!"

Ronnie surveyed his sister with something like alarm.

"Good grief! Do you know what you're talking about? How

116

do you know Mums wants to go off by herself? Or Grandma Lane either, for that matter? Not everyone wants a change."

All she meant was that everyone should have a chance to find out what he or she wanted, Jane argued. Grandma Lane might not care—after doing the same thing for a hundred years, one might not care to try anything new, she conceded.

"But I think we ought to encourage Mums to—to be a little reckless, though what I really mean is, I think, to be a little selfish. I've thought for a long time, and I'm sure I'm right," said Jane modestly, "that selfishness is not as character wrecking as people believe. Be selfish—in a nice way, of course—and you will be happy. That's my motto!"

"Got it all thought out, haven't you?" Ronnie gazed at his twin in some astonishment. "At that, you know, I think you may be right."

"Of course I'm right," Jane agreed. "But how we're going to break Mums of the habit of always putting the family first is a different matter."

A few days later she announced complacently that the "problem" had been solved.

"I was talking to Grandpa Lane about it, and he said that women are funny," Jane reported. "They have to have an incentive—only he called it an excuse—for doing anything they really like, I mean enjoy doing. Now he takes the bus and goes into town as often as he pleases and just 'looks around,' as he calls it. But would Mums do that?"

Her mother, Jane said, as Ronnie looked puzzled, would need to have some kind of errand to do—an appointment with the dentist, or perhaps getting Ronnie some new socks.

"Grandma Lane is like that, too. Can you imagine her taking off just to have some fun? She'd worry every minute that she might be late getting back and dinner wouldn't be ready on time."

Ronnie said, "I see what you mean, but how the heck can we do anything to change their minds?"

Grandpa Lane, Jane answered, was for some reason enthusiastically in favor of having his wife and Jane's mother "get out of the house and enjoy the fresh air." Jane rather thought that he planned to eat an extra large slice of banana cream pie in their absence, but that would be on his conscience, not hers.

"He loves to rummage in the fridge," Jane said. "There's a certain kind of nail he says he has to have, and the idea is to get Mums and Grandma Lane to go into Acton and get a box of them. The catch is that they are not manufactured any more—no hardware store carries them. But, he says, Grandpa Lane says, that once women get where the shops are, wild horses can't drive them away."

Any doubts Ronnie might have had concerning this reasoning were dispelled at breakfast the next morning. She and Grandma Lane, his mother announced, planned to go shopping in Acton. They might see a movie in the afternoon, but whatever they did, they would be home in time to have dinner ready at the usual hour.

"A little fresh air will be good for you," Grandpa Lane assured them kindly.

His wife eyed him suspiciously. "The real reason we're going is to get you those nails," she reminded him. "There's plenty of fresh air just outside this house."

Miles Hubbard, intercepting a warning glance from his wife, said hastily that everyone appreciated a change of scene.

"You got enough money, Liz?" he asked his wife.

"Don't call me Liz. Of course I have enough money," she replied, in the absent tone of the woman trying to remember where she has put her secret shopping list. "Can I get you anything, dear?"

The twins' voices drowned their father's negative. This was not to be a shopping trip for the family, they reminded their mother. In fact, if she brought home *anything*, except for herself, she could count on having it returned. Fortunately no one observed the exchange of nervous glances between the two old people, and breakfast ended in what might be called an atmosphere of amiable anticipation.

An hour later the "fresh-air seekers," as Jane had dubbed them, were ready to be escorted to the bus stop. Grandma Lane improved the opportunity to warn her husband that the cream pie was for dinner dessert and that a tempting light lunch had been left for him in the refrigerator.

"He'll eat the pie, of course," she remarked philosophically, when seated in the bus. "In fact, it's not too much to say he wouldn't have encouraged me to take a day off if I'd left him only a rice pudding. Men," concluded Grandma Lane, "are funny."

Acton was pleasantly alive, with fairly crowded walks and streets lined at the curbs with parked cars. The early-April sun was warm, but a sharp wind caught the unwary at street intersections, and most pedestrians, men included, still wore winter coats. The main shopping area covered four or five blocks; smaller places, such as hardware stores, tended to prefer the side streets. Food stores were more widely scattered, and Grandma Lane, an inveterate comparison shopper, could not pass one of these without halting to study the window displays for price signs.

They conscientiously tried four hardware shops in search of the nail Grandpa Lane had requested, and were told in each place that it had not been manufactured for many years. In fact, one earnest young clerk assured them, they held in their hands a veritable curiosity that might, in the future, be of value to a collector or a museum.

"Well, that's that," Elizabeth Hubbard said briskly, after the fourth shop had confirmed this pronouncement. "We ought to have lunch early, if we're going to the movies."

The question of where to eat was quickly settled. She had harbored a secret desire for years, Grandma Lane confided, to eat at a drugstore fountain. People always seemed to be having such a good time over their food in such places, and they were early enough—it was half past eleven—to be able to avoid a crowd.

Her companion laughed her delightful contralto laugh, which made several passers-by glance at her appreciatively.

"When I think of the lectures I've read the twins about spending their lunch money on that kind of stuff—well, I blush," she said. "However, as you say, it will be a change."

The length of the sandwich list bewildered Grandma Lane, but the small, thin, incredibly swift-moving young girl behind the counter had had experience in helping the indecisive to make up their minds. The "shoppers' special," she said, was very good.

"It saves you time," she pointed out—time, in her experience, being more valuable than digestion.

Elizabeth Hubbard, also urged to have the shoppers' special, acquiesced, and the two women had almost finished before the stools on either side of them were occupied. A middle-aged woman seated herself next to Grandma Lane, and a young man who looked like a student took the stool on Elizabeth Hubbard's left.

"Take my advice and avoid the shoppers' special," he said out of the side of his mouth. "Bacon and tomato, isn't it? It's been that for the last six weeks."

She laughed, and he grinned at her cheerfully.

Grandma Lane was fumbling in her purse for change.

"What was the dessert?" the newcomer asked her, frankly

trying to appraise the few crumbs left on the small dessert plate.

"Marble cake!" Grandma Lane answered, in a voice that must have been audible throughout the store. "And believe me, that's the name for it—like a rock. But the coffee," she added, in the same clear tone, "was better than I expected."

She was only answering the woman's question, she said defensively when, once they were out on the street, Elizabeth Hubbard, still scarlet-faced, reproached her. No, it wasn't the poor little counter-girl's fault; she knew that and had left her a quarter.

"But that cake must have been two weeks old—somebody ought to speak up in a case like that."

There was no use in arguing about it, Elizabeth Hubbard conceded, but she had never been so embarrassed in her life. She doubted that she could ever go into that drugstore again.

A wholly unrepentant Grandma Lane remarked that there was no use in spoiling the afternoon, and were they going to the movies or not?

"Why don't we just do some shopping?" Elizabeth Hubbard suggested. "Aside from being expensive—that theater on the next street wants three dollars—all the pictures advertised seem to be pretty lurid. Why don't we find out if any of the stores are having sales today?"

For the next two hours they pushed their way through crowds, in and out of department stores and specialty shops, and even in one instance joined the rapt circle of bemused spectators fascinated by a street display of small rugs smuggled, they were told, past the customhouse. As Elizabeth Hubbard whispered, it was a relief to be able to stare at something they neither needed nor wanted without being told so by an irritated husband.

"Men never see any sense in just looking," Grandma Lane

murmured, gazing raptly at a fringed atrocity. "They buy the first thing they see, and usually it's all wrong."

By four o'clock the shoppers had each accumulated a capacious string bag full of small packages. Weariness was beginning to take its toll, although etiquette dictated a firm denial. A cup of tea before boarding the return bus was allowable, and it was just before they entered an attractive tearoom on a side street that Elizabeth made the alarming discovery that her wallet was missing from her bag.

"Someone's taken it!" she gasped. "My credit cards, too. All I have left are two pennies in my change purse."

Grandma Lane turned a stricken face toward her.

"I haven't any money!" She held out her open purse in pathetic evidence. "Not even a penny."

She had "just spent it," she explained, in answer to Elizabeth's questions. No, a pickpocket couldn't be blamed. It had taken her last dollar bill and all her change to pay for a necktie she had bought for her husband.

"He's like a child—it means a lot to him when I bring him something from downtown."

Elizabeth Hubbard was conscious that her back ached. There seemed to be no place to sit down. It might not be too late to reach Miles at his office, or Reade, but both carfare and phone calls required money. She had no idea how far they were from her husband's office, and now she recalled that Reade Coleman had said that he expected to be out of the city all day and might not be back for dinner. There would be no use in trying to get in touch with him.

"I suppose we could pawn something?" Grandma Lane appeared to be perfectly serious.

That was the result of years of light reading, Elizabeth Hubbard thought. But she hesitated to offer her own solution—that they try to walk home. It wouldn't kill them, she had decided, if they walked slowly, but Grandma Lane might collapse somewhere on the deserted road.

"I think we'd better ask for bus fare," she said, far more confidently than she felt. "We'll promise to mail back the money."

"You mean *beg?*" Grandma Lane quavered. "I never begged for anything in all my life."

This was an emergency, Elizabeth reminded her. It was worth trying, at least.

"I'll take one side of the street and you take the other," she proposed. "Just ask for bus fare. It's nothing to be ashamed of."

But to herself she made a vow that hereafter she would never reject a plea for alms regardless of the excuse, or lack of excuse.

"Could you—" She attempted to intercept a young man, who, briefcase swinging, dashed against her.

He muttered an apology and fled on.

Two bundle-laden women, walking slowly toward her, merely stared when she asked, in a low voice, for bus fare. They said nothing, but stepped around her, one on each side.

Elizabeth wondered about Grandma Lane—certainly the plight of a white-haired old woman should make some impression.

"Please, could you let me—" Elizabeth this time tackled an elderly gentleman, prosperity in every line of his immaculate raiment. He looked at her in extreme distaste, removed his cigar from his mouth long enough to say, "You must have had one too many," and walked on.

The five o'clock homeward rush was well started, and Elizabeth instinctively kept to the curb line to avoid the unrelenting pressure. She was relieved to see Grandma Lane being piloted across the street by a large and kindly policeman.

"She almost got herself run over," he said, steering the old lady toward Elizabeth. "You know her? Good—take care of her."

Grandma Lane watched his retreating back, until she judged it safe to whisper. She had stopped only one person, she said, a young colored woman who had given her a dime but had hurried on before she could be asked her name and address.

"If I drop dead, right here in the streets, I simply can't keep on asking," she declared. "I feel awful, right now."

"I know, it's terrible," Elizabeth comforted her. "I wonder—"

She broke off to watch a rather shabby youth who had suddenly emerged from the crowd and was evidently prepared to drive off in the car parked directly in front of the two women.

"I beg your pardon." Elizabeth's voice trembled slightly. "Could you—I mean would you—is it asking too much of you to give us a lift?"

The young man, already seated in the car, stared at her in astonishment, but he did not close the car door.

"Bus line broke down?" he leered.

Grandma Lane shifted a heavy shopping bag from one hand to the other. "We haven't any money," she quavered, and for a moment her companion realized how they must look to the motorist—two well-dressed elderly women, laden with the evident spoils of a shopping spree. She could even anticipate the derisive "Oh, yea?" of the shabby youth.

But he surprised her by asking where they wanted to go, and, their address given, slid out from behind the wheel.

"Okay, it sounds crazy all right," he muttered. "Here, give me your bags—good Lord, you musta been buying out the town!"

Before they could grasp his intention, he had seized their shopping bags, tossed them into the rear of the car, slid back behind the wheel, and started the car. He was off before the two women left standing on the curb could open their mouths to scream.

Elizabeth Hubbard was the first to recover. She glanced at her hands clutching only her gloves.

"Well, at least he didn't knock us down," she said, and then, realizing that they themselves had confessed their poverty, she laughed hysterically. "I wonder if he'll appreciate that bargain box of toothbrushes," she murmured.

Grandma Lane said fretfully that there was never a policeman around when he was needed—the universal complaint of the average American citizen. She presented a forlorn picture, hugging her worn purse to her breast and trembling slightly from shock.

A woman passer-by stopped to ask if they had taken the car's number.

"I was about half a block away," she explained, "and I saw him grab your parcels. You should have yelled, or at least got his number."

Not, she assured them, barely waiting for their reply in the negative, that it would have done them much good. The thief was most likely driving a stolen car or had rigged up false license plates. After a few sympathetic clucks she left them, and it was not until she had turned the next corner and was out of sight that it occurred to either of them that she might have been willing to lend them bus fare.

They were debating their next move when a somewhat guttural voice coming from behind them made them jump. Their already tense nerves were not soothed by the sight of a short, squarely built man, who beamed at them cheerily. He was well dressed, hatless, and definitely smelled of strong drink, an impression that his fixed, vacant smile did nothing to dispel.

"Be of good faith," he said solemnly, speaking with a decided accent. "Let us be friends. No?"

"Yes, of course," Elizabeth Hubbard answered hurriedly,

conscious that Grandma Lane was trying to hide behind her.

The man took a step toward her and lowered his voice to a confidential whisper. "You wish to go home?" he inquired.

With difficulty Elizabeth Hubbard managed to stifle an inclination to add "Alive!" but contented herself with a brief nod.

He had a car, the stranger revealed. If they wished, he would take them. Providing they promised to—he suddenly abandoned his attempt to communicate in English and lapsed into what sounded like a mixture of the Latin languages.

". . . sleep" was one distinguishable word, followed by something that Grandma Lane later interpreted as "for the night."

"He wants a place to sleep for the night," the old lady translated compassionately. "Tell him it's all right—he can have the first-floor room—if he gives us a lift home."

This message, relayed, was received with enthusiasm. He had parked his car, obviously second- or thirdhand and in need of repair, on a side street, and he led his passengers to it, talking volubly, and oblivious, once the car was reached, of any amenities. He seated himself behind the wheel and left them to open the rear door and climb unassisted into the dusty interior.

"How much do you think he's had to drink?" Grandma Lane whispered, when they narrowly missed sideswiping a parked car.

He wasn't drunk, Elizabeth Hubbard pointed out dubiously, but what worried her was the task of explaining him to the family at home. She was not, she observed with rising agitation, in the habit of bringing home perfectly strange men to dinner.

The necessity for keeping their voices low hampered conversation, and Elizabeth's nervousness increased, until by the time the house was reached she heartily wished they had at-

tempted to walk the distance home, rather than trust themselves to this peculiar character.

"This the house?" The character startled her by the
abruptness of the question.

It was dark by this time, and lights twinkled merrily from the
windows. How on earth am I going to explain him? Elizabeth
thought wildly. But her voice was steady as she said yes, this
was the house, and would he come in and meet her husband?

Again the man made no effort to help them out of the car,
but tramped doggedly and silently after them as they walked
toward the house. The porch light went on suddenly, and the
hall door opened to release a hospitable flood of welcoming
brightness.

"We'd begun to worry about you." Jane's young voice altered. "Oh!"

Elizabeth said, "Where's your father?" and heard the door
behind her close.

Miles Hubbard and Reade Coleman came out of the living
room. Of course it would have to be a night when they were
home early, Elizabeth told herself in exasperation.

"This is Mr.—er—er—" She floundered, too late realizing
that she had not asked the man his name. "My husband, Mr.
Hubbard, and his friend Mr. Coleman."

A faint movement at the top of the stairs told her that Victoria May was probably listening. Mercifully, Ronnie and the
children were absent. And Grandpa Lane must be in the
kitchen.

"He very kindly brought us home," Elizabeth plodded on.
Why didn't the idiot supply his name? "He's staying for dinner
and overnight. I'll tell you what happened to us after we eat."

But the stranger, his small, dark eyes darting suspiciously
around the circle of faces, took a step backward that brought
him up against the door.

"No, I am not staying," he growled. "All I ask is where is a bar. My friend keeps it. The lady was going to take me—so she said. This is no bar."

"You said you wanted a place to sleep." Grandma Lane, her courage restored by familiar surroundings, spoke severely.

He could sleep in Luigi's place, the man muttered. No, he did not want a hot supper. And they could keep their blank blank money.

Suddenly he began to scream.

"You keep your hands off me!" he shrieked. "And do not call the police, or I'll—"

The remainder of the threat was lost in the slam of the front door, and a moment later the car was heard to start.

"He'll come back!" Grandma Lane prophesied. "He'll come back and murder us in our beds!"

This possibility provided an exciting topic of conversation during dinner and throughout the evening. The twins— Ronnie, bitterly disappointed to have missed the stranger, insisted on taking what he said were fingerprints off the front doorknob—were all for staying awake throughout the night and were with difficulty dissuaded from setting booby traps in the first-floor rooms. The man couldn't do much harm if he never got above the first floor, they argued.

Victoria May declared her intention of sitting up all night, and the children, before they were hustled off to bed, offered their services as watchmen.

"Wednesday is all the protection we'll need," Miles Hubbard said, patting the dog's head as it rested on his knee. "I doubt if Mr. Er-er would even be able to find his way back here after he's found his favorite bar."

But to his wife Miles admitted that he didn't dare take chances where an unbalanced man was concerned.

"There's just a chance that he may come back, so Reade and I will spell each other from eleven to six. Reade doesn't have to be at his office before noon tomorrow, so he'll take the two-thirty-to-six watch."

Neither of the men expected any real trouble, but, they assured each other, the women might develop a bad case of the jitters unless convinced of adequate protection. Fortunately the night hours were routinely peaceful, and a few minutes after six, his guard duty accomplished, Reade was pondering whether it was worth the trouble of returning to bed before he could expect breakfast to be ready, when he was startled by a tremendous clatter of what sounded like tin pans. A stream of profanity provided a kind of obbligato.

"What the hell!" The young milkman glowered fiercely at Reade, who stared at him around the edge of the half-opened door.

"What was that racket?" Reade demanded, in the voice of a justly indignant householder. "You want to wake up the entire neighborhood? It's only six o'clock."

The milkman had a voice that carried. "What's the big idea?" he demanded. "I'm setting down six quarts of milk— 'Leave the milk out front,' the note says—and before I can get up the steps I walk into a wire that knocks down a mess of pots and pans. If you ask me, someone's gone loony."

"What happened?" Grandma Lane inquired fearfully, from behind Reade. "What was all that noise?"

Before Reade could answer, Ronnie slid down the banisters and shot past Reade out into the open. Jane was close behind him. They greeted the scowling milkman as a long-lost friend.

"Pay it no mind, Jake," Ronnie advised him kindly. "We were trying to trap a suspicious character, that's all. Not your fault—you know how these things happen."

Jane was less conciliatory. "I thought you left the milk at the back door," she said.

The milkman reiterated that a note had instructed him to

leave the milk "out front." He couldn't waste all day arguing, he grumbled; he was late now. And he would appreciate it if they would make up their minds where they wanted milk delivered and would stick to the decision.

After he had left, momentarily subdued, the twins offered to take Wednesday for a walk before breakfast. The three children, only half dressed, clamored to go with them, but Jane, usually susceptible to pleading, refused them firmly.

"Now and then I get tired of little pitchers," she said to Ronnie, when they were out of sight of the house. "Everybody needs a little time to think. Shall we leave Wednesday off the leash?"

It was so early there could be no danger in letting the dog run free for a couple of blocks, Ronnie thought. He glanced at his sister shrewdly. "Something on your mind?" he asked.

"Well, yes." Jane hesitated. "It's something Bertha told me. She tells me things because she says I don't lose my mind and yell. Not that Mother ever yells, but she does get excited."

Ronnie asked diplomatically if whatever Bertha had said could be called a yelling matter.

"Well, it's about that revolver." Jane spoke rapidly. "You know, the one Robert found and the police have now. Bertha says it belongs to her husband."

Bertha was the woman-by-the-day who came in three times a week to do the cleaning.

No, as far as she knew Bertha's husband had had no plans for holding up the family, Jane said, in answer to Ronnie's questions. And it wasn't the husband who had hidden the revolver in the bushes—Bertha herself had done that.

"But the thing was loaded!" Ronnie protested. "Didn't she know that Robert would probably find it? He's always poking around. Suppose it had gone off and killed him?"

Bertha had worried about that afterward, Jane said.

"In fact, it was because she was afraid that it might go off that she hid it. She isn't going to tell her husband that it's been found—what he doesn't know won't upset him, she says."

"Upset him!" Ronnie repeated. "It's too bad about him. What's she going to tell him when he misses his little toy?"

Bertha's husband was not likely to miss the revolver, Jane said calmly. He had plenty more—in fact, he had a "kind of" collection of firearms. "Anyway," she added brightly, "that solves the mystery."

It would be just as well, she admitted, not to discuss the subject with the family, although if any questions were asked—their father, the twins agreed, would be the one most likely to ask—they would of course explain. But Ronnie, whistling for Wednesday and turning to walk back, silently wondered how many revolvers Bertha's husband had collected if the loss of one would not be noticed.

9

Victoria and her hair were becoming something of a problem in the household routine. Anxious to save money, Victoria had resorted to home shampoos; but, as she herself admitted, she lacked the knack, and her fine, thin hair resisted all her efforts to coax it to conform. Fortunately or unfortunately, Jane Hubbard could "do anything" with the crowning glory, her own or another's. In Jane's clever fingers the rollers magically produced firm, smooth curls that, under her manipulation of the brush and comb, were transformed into beautiful, natural-looking waves. Not even Suzette's highest-priced operators, Victoria testified (and she had tried them all), could make her hair look as lovely as Jane could. It would be a criminal waste of talent, Victoria declared passionately, if Jane's future did not include a beauty shop of her own.

The attitude of Jane's mother genuinely puzzled Victoria.

Apparently she had no objections to Jane's doing Victoria's hair, or Grandma Lane's, but no regular schedule must be set up, and Jane must not accept any payment. Her skill must be offered as a favor.

The insistence on nonpayment irked Victoria. Not only did she feel the child deserved recompense, but, too, services paid for entitled the payee to make definite demands and would instill a sense of obligation in those who served. Elizabeth Hubbard, Victoria thought, missed a good many opportunities to instill.

She had gone up to her room to put on a bathrobe and was collecting the essentials for her shampoo when she noticed that the bottle of liquid soap was missing—a special and expensive brand that she devoutly believed was essential to the health of her hair.

Convinced that "someone" had borrowed it, she searched the cabinets in the other bathrooms, but found no trace of the black-and-gold bottle. She could hear Grandma Lane and Elizabeth Hubbard talking on the first floor, and she leaned over the banister and called to them.

"A bottle of shampoo?" Elizabeth Hubbard repeated her question. "Why no, I don't think so, Vicky. Where would it be if it was where it ought to be?"

The shampoo bottle, Victoria said very distinctly, belonged on the second shelf of the cabinet in the third-floor bathroom. No, she most certainly had not used it up and forgotten to lay in a fresh supply—she might observe, Victoria reminded her hearers, that she was not exactly feeble-minded. The shampoo was missing, and someone must have taken it.

"It probably was Bertha," she suggested, trying to whisper and yet at the same time be clearly heard.

"Oh, do hush!" Elizabeth Hubbard frowned at the figure leaning over the railing. "Why on earth would she want the stuff? You've forgotten where you put it, that's all."

Victoria, she said to herself, was forever mislaying her possessions and was only too ready to accuse Bertha. But also, being a fair-minded woman, she admitted that it was a tendency of many employers to question the honesty of those they employed.

"I've plenty of good Castile shampoo. Use as much as you like," she offered cheerfully. "And I forgot to tell you—the hot water will be shut off for most of tomorrow morning. The plumber's coming to do something to the boiler. So it's a good thing you decided to do your hair this afternoon."

She never used anything but Balm Supreme on her hair, Victoria replied. And it was bad enough not to have the proper shampoo on hand without being obliged to do everything herself.

"I must say I think it would have been more gracious of Jane to have told me she was going off on some wild-goose chase. She knows how much I depend on her to help. But then, the young have no consideration."

Whether Elizabeth Hubbard's rule, when ruffled, to "count ten" before she spoke could have been maintained was not to be tested. Grandma Lane, breathing heavily, appeared in the doorway of the dining room.

"All the bath towels are gone!" she announced. "And the pink bath mat, too."

The first-floor bathroom, at the end of the hall, was especially convenient for the children and for Grandpa Lane, in his role as gardener. Victoria tied the cord of her robe more tightly and hurried down the stairs, proclaiming at every step that she had always known "it" would happen. Half hysterically, she declined to explain what she meant by "it," but her nervousness was not assumed, and Elizabeth Hubbard put a comforting arm around her.

Grandma Lane was of the generation that puts its trust in

the strength and wisdom of man. She had already summoned her husband from his labors, and he was coming in the door as Victoria gained the hall. Afterward he assured her that working in the sun had affected his eyes, but, whatever the reason, at his first sight of her he gulped.

"Great God Almighty! What happened to you?" he demanded.

Victoria's rather erratic sense of humor saved the situation. Her hair, standing up all over her head in stiff red spikes, was the result of a new treatment, she explained, and actually giggled.

"I suppose I look like the top of an iron fence after being scraped with rust remover," she said affably. "It'll come off all right—don't worry."

Grandma Lane said hurriedly that she thought he ought to know that some sort of burglar was roaming through the house and, as the only man at home, his duty was to run down and capture the thief. At the same time, she warned anxiously that the man might have a knife or a gun, and would Caspar please be careful?

"Well, where is he?" Grandpa Lane evidently regarded this as a sensible question and was unprepared for the scornful retort that that was what he was supposed to find out.

The second question, had the burglar taken anything, was equally foolish, from a wifely point of view. Of course he had stolen something—that was what made him a burglar.

"He's stolen my bottle of shampoo," Victoria testified.

"Yes, and what's more, he's taken all the towels out of the bathroom!" Grandma Lane's agitation increased. "All of them. The big bath towels and the face towels, even the washcloths."

She hadn't the slightest idea why a thief would be interested in *towels*, she snapped, brushing aside her husband's astonished question. The towels were missing, the thief was probably prowling the house in search of other booty, and what did Caspar intend to do about it?

The old man was saved from having to answer by the sudden appearance of Holly, followed by Leila and Robert, dragging Wednesday after them. All three children were dripping wet, and Holly carried a blue bath towel on which she tripped at every other step.

"Look!" they cried in unison. "Look! Wednesday's all clean. We shampooed him!"

The bedraggled dog, tail between his legs, was a picture of abject misery. His coat appeared to be covered with some sticky substance, and at intervals he moaned.

Confronted by the four adults, the procession halted. Leila and Robert exchanged anxious glances, but Holly pirouetted airily.

"We washed him," she announced.

Grandpa Lane put his hand on the dog's head and made an instant discovery.

"He's covered with soap! You haven't rinsed it off, and it's a wonder you haven't blinded the poor animal."

Robert, as usual, seemed to be the elected spokesman. They had not rinsed off the soap, he explained, because this was the kind of soap you wiped off.

"It leaves the hair soft and silky," he said, evidently quoting some remembered advertisement. "Besides," he admitted, "we didn't have any water."

Elizabeth Hubbard spoke quickly. Where, she asked, had the children found the soap?

"We borrowed it," Robert revealed. "From Aunt Vicky."

Victoria's cry of anguish was real. The shampoo, she screamed, cost seven dollars a bottle, and to think of it being poured out on a dog! This came from letting the children run wild; no one in the house paid the slightest attention to disciplining them.

The undisciplined three gazed at her with concern. After a moment Robert muttered that he had not thought it would matter so much. He would buy her another bottle, he assured the weeping Victoria. To her retort that he had no money, he reminded her that he indeed did have money—in his bank.

"What about the towels?" Grandma Lane interrupted this dialogue. "You took all the towels from the bathroom, and this blue one is all you've brought back."

You couldn't trust Holly, Robert sighed, like one burdened with responsibility. He had gathered up the towels and given them to Holly to carry, but she must have dropped some and not bothered to pick them up.

The idea of Holly leaving a trail of towels behind her suggested a question simultaneously to Elizabeth Hubbard and Grandma Lane: where, they asked, had the children given Wednesday his bath? To which Robert answered that the vacant lot across the street had been selected as an ideal place.

"We didn't want to upset you," he explained politely.

What to do about children who borrowed things without asking would be decided after dinner that night, Elizabeth Hubbard told him. Meanwhile he was to retrieve the missing towels, and Leila and Holly were to take baths. Grandpa Lane volunteered to rinse off poor Wednesday, and the result was that for the rest of the day the dog wafted a wave of expensive perfume each time he stirred.

"It's all because they haven't enough to do," Grandma Lane said, her tone strongly disapproving. "In my day children were expected to help around the house. Especially on Saturdays."

Victoria agreed. The modern trend accented all activities outside the home, to the extent that the modern child had come to regard his home as little more than a boardinghouse.

"Well, I want to make it perfectly clear," she declared, waving her hairbrush for emphasis, "that when I take my vacation I intend to work on my book. I'll be here, of course, but I am not to be at the beck and call of *anyone.*"

"If no one should call her to come to meals, I'll bet she would raise Cain," Grandpa Lane observed, when Victoria had closed the bathroom door. "Do her good to lend a hand with weeding the garden," he added solemnly. "She's been putting on weight lately."

The question of vacations increasingly dominated the dinner-table conversation. Young couples—as the Lanes carefully explained, more or less distantly related—had apparently come to regard them as trustworthy baby-sitters available throughout the vacation season. To find them fully occupied, and evidently in funds, was a situation that required detailed explanation. Grandma Lane was only too ready to furnish particulars and not at all reluctant to show her satisfaction. For the first time in years, she confided to Elizabeth Hubbard, she felt free to devote her attention to making strawberry jam.

Rather to their surprise, the Hubbards learned that their usual plan of sending the twins to camp did not meet with Miss Mary's program for summer family life. Elizabeth Hubbard, who had hitherto regarded a well-run summer camp as a lifesaver for parents, was told that camps were only one more modern excuse for discarding parental responsibility. The accent must be on family living the year 'round.

"Of course, the poor dear doesn't know what it is to live with two rioting teen-agers the year 'round," Elizabeth Hubbard reminded her husband. "Well, at least I won't have to worry about them being drowned in the camp lake," she concluded cheerily. And when Victoria, with her usual absence of tact, suggested that it was possible for the twins to drown in the artificial lake supported by the city, she retorted that that was beside the question.

She was totally unprepared for the confrontation with Jane and Ronnie early the following week. The twins, who found her placidly shelling peas on the tiny back porch, had been to the Acton library and were laden with books.

"We took everyone's list," Ronnie said, letting books tumble from his arms onto the lowest step. "And Jane snared the new Thomas Bevis for you, Mums."

Jane deposited her load on the top step near her mother's feet. Wednesday, asleep across the kitchen entrance, opened one eye and wagged his tail, but evidently decided not to interrupt his afternoon nap.

"We saw Miss Parker in the library, Mums," Ronnie said. "She asked about you. Said to tell you she misses having lunch with you at Fuller's."

Jane had seated herself on the step, her back against a post. She eyed her mother speculatively, one hand tugging at a lock of her long red hair.

"She said something kind of funny, Mums." Jane hesitated. "When she asked how you were and we said fine, she said, 'A lot you know about your mother.' Kind of sarcastic, wasn't it, Ronnie?"

Her brother nodded. "But she's a friend of yours, isn't she, Mums?"

"Yes, of course." Elizabeth Hubbard nodded. "I haven't seen her in ages. We used to have lunch together, two or three times a month."

Miss Parker had made the same remark, Jane reported. Both twins thought that she had looked at them "funnylike," Ronnie said.

"As if we'd been stealing the family silver, or something," Jane explained. "Anyway, I'm dead sure she doesn't approve of us."

Elizabeth Hubbard dismissed this statement as pure guesswork, but late that afternoon, when dinner preparations were absorbing her attention and that of Grandma Lane, Cordelia Parker telephoned.

With the deliberation of the woman whose dinner problems are automatically solved for her by any one of a half-dozen better restaurants, Miss Parker proceeded leisurely to re-establish rapport. It was, she regretted, so fatally easy to lose touch with one's friends in the crowded city life. The sight of Elizabeth's children—positively grown up!—had at once amazed and alarmed her.

"I didn't like to ask personal questions," Miss Parker stated, without tripping on a word, "but of course I was dying to hear news of you. Where are you working now, dear?"

Well, of course, it was the homebodies who kept the world revolving, Miss Parker admitted, but without conviction. Everyone agreed that the Home was the nation's cornerstone. The great pity was that so few women could afford to stay at home—in fact, she seemed to remember that Elizabeth Hubbard had two children almost ready for college—"and we all know how expensive tuition is these days. Not to mention board and laundry and . . ."

Elizabeth Hubbard had had a great deal of practical experience in postponing personal reflections until her time was free. She usually had a few moments to herself following dinner and before the "family" came together in the living room. Tonight, she deliberately lingered over the rites of freshening up, and seated herself in the small rocking chair in her bedroom, taking the precaution first to turn off the light. Something Cordelia Parker had said was disturbing, and if she could have just a few minutes in which to sort over her thoughts . . .

The reason she had gone back to office work, once the twins were in high school and no longer came home at noon for lunch, had been to earn and save money for their education.

Neither she nor her husband was a college graduate, and at rare intervals she found herself in agreement with Grandma Lane, who frankly proclaimed that she thought "anyone" could make an honest living without having a college diploma. When pressed to be explicit, the old lady reluctantly admitted that the twins were not likely to be satisfied to make an honest living unless the work also provided opportunities for advancement.

Well, the college fund was practically assured now, Elizabeth Hubbard reflected, rocking gently. Miss Mary Hall had been more than generous in the matter of salaries, and the Hubbards' savings account was steadily increasing. And yet—and yet—

She had supposed her only reason for returning to business had been to further the education of her children. Certainly Miles had thought so: he made no secret of the fact that one of the main reasons for his acceptance of his role in Miss Mary's plan was that, for the year at least, it would not be necessary for his wife to work. But was there something more behind the popular and ever-ready excuse of the middle-aged woman for holding fast to her job?

If I'm honest, thought Elizabeth Hubbard, who at the moment disdained to shrink from self-examination, I must admit that I miss the office life. I miss getting out of the house every morning and not coming back till night; the things I wanted to do and didn't have time to do don't interest me now that I *do* have the time. Probably it's always the way!

It must have been all the chatter about vacations that explained her moping, she decided, rising and automatically reaching for the perfume spray. When she felt "down," she usually found her favorite violet scent comforting. Everyone who went to business looked forward to a vacation as a matter of course—only housewives like herself and Grandma Lane were expected to stay put the year 'round. In her altered status, Elizabeth thought ruefully, it would be silly to plan a vacation—or wouldn't it?

Downstairs she found them all apparently occupied and content. Grandma Lane knitting, Grandpa reading the evening paper on the other side of the round table. Miles Hubbard and Reade Coleman were playing chess, the twins doing homework in the alcove. The three children, on the floor before the fireplace—the evenings were still damp and cold enough to make a fire pleasant—were waiting expectantly, each holding a small, shabby book.

"Read!" they chorused as Elizabeth Hubbard entered the room. Leila added a late and beguiling "Please?"

It was Elizabeth's theory that by persuading them to listen politely to each one's choice some faint trace of courtesy or unselfishness might be absorbed, but her theories were usually quickly discarded in favor of peace terms. Tonight, she pointed out, it was Holly's turn to have "first choice."

"And if you wrangle over it too long, it will be bedtime before you hear a word," Elizabeth warned.

The books on child training, as Jane, who read them all, had informed her, instructed that under no circumstances must a child be threatened.

"Persuasion and explanation are the key words," Jane had explained.

Grandma Lane was perhaps the shrewdest observer in the circle, and Elizabeth's restlessness had not escaped her attention. Beyond the stereotyped "You ought to get out of the house more," the older woman had made no comment, but this evening, after the children were in bed, she managed to direct the conversation to women's clubs.

"I think they're a good thing," she announced, with some emphasis. "Not that I ever belonged to one, or ever shall."

Elizabeth Hubbard did not look up from her needlework—she was hemming new table napkins. "A waste of good time," she said.

Not always and not all of them, Grandma protested. Club-women had earned the respect of the City Council and other political bodies. They had backed many worth-while measures, and they numbered enough to have their votes regarded with respect.

"I've been urging Mums to join the Acton Ladies' Literary Club for ages," Jane said unexpectedly. "They really work."

Any organization with a name like that could not appeal to her, Elizabeth protested. The members probably read their own effusions to each other at every meeting.

"You see, you make up your mind before you find out the facts," Jane scolded. "That silly name doesn't mean a thing. The club was founded fifty years ago and the name sticks. But no member is literary now—"

"She means no member is a lady," Ronnie contributed, ducking as his sister whirled on him.

"No, but I'm serious, Mums," she insisted. "The—the *women* work for the hospital, and keep track of the City Council, and get a lot done. They really do."

But I don't want to do good works, Elizabeth's silent protests continued. I want to be part of the commercial world—where an office is impersonal and yet no one is isolated.

10

If they couldn't go to camp for the summer vacation, would there be any objection, the twins asked, to their serving as counselors in a day camp established in Acton for underprivileged children? This suggestion met with enthusiastic approval, only Victoria voicing the hope that all the campers would be vaccinated. Reassured on this point, she not only gave her approval, but also contributed ten dollars to the camp's weekly ice cream fund.

Grandpa Lane, moved to speech one evening early in July, astonished the family group by suggesting that Miles Hubbard and Reade Coleman might both spend their vacations working in the garden. By this time Grandpa Lane's efforts had far exceeded not only his own expectations, but also those of the other adults. The only criticism that could be leveled at the proud gardener was that he seemed to favor an excessive planting of onions, but this vegetable, as his loyal wife pointed out, was indispensable to the good cook.

Weeding onions, or, for that matter, any kind of vegetable, was not his idea of rest and change, Reade Coleman said bluntly. And Miles Hubbard testified with some fervor that one reason he had left the farm on which he was born was the amount of weeding needed to produce a teaspoonful of food. He regarded the supermarket as a back saver, and he, for one, didn't begrudge a cent of what it charged.

Reade would have liked to take off in his car for what he vaguely described as "the wilds," and he had tentatively suggested that he and Miles disappear together. He was even willing to promise that they would put up at a hotel every night if Miles shuddered at the thought of washing a pot or pan. But, to his exasperation, Miles stubbornly insisted that he intended to adhere to Miss Mary's exactions.

"A vacation has to be a family affair," Miles reiterated. "You know that's the understanding. In the good old days—"

In the good old days, he was reminded, families had summer homes, either at the shore or in the country, and amusement and occupation presented no problems.

"Except to the women," Grandma Lane interrupted quickly. "Three meals a day was still the rule, wasn't it?"

Elizabeth Hubbard took a deep breath. "Do you know what my idea of a vacation is?" she asked dreamily. "To eat dinner out every night for a week."

Her husband stared incredulously. "Every night for a week?" he repeated. "Why, where would you go, Liz?"

It needn't be a different restaurant each time, she assured him. The menus would be varied. "And don't call me Liz," she added.

Unexpectedly her husband laughed. He had been thinking,

merely thinking, he said, that after a day spent doing odd jobs around the house—and from past experience he had learned that a home vacation always included innumerable small jobs—a good steak dinner put a man in the proper frame of mind to enjoy a well-earned evening of leisure.

The next night, he and Reade were greeted by the information that Miss Mary, with the vacation season in mind, had sent the half-dozen large packages that nearly filled the front hall.

"We wanted everyone to be here before we opened any," Elizabeth Hubbard explained. "The children are nearly exploding with curiosity."

Dinner could wait, they all agreed, and as the two men worked with hammer and screw driver the atmosphere of surprise deepened to such a point that Holly was convinced she had narrowly missed seeing Santa Claus.

The first box yielded a handsome croquet set. It had been at least fifty years since she had played croquet, Grandma Lane said, holding one of the balls tenderly in her wrinkled hands.

The second box contained the parts for a lawn swing and the third a colorful hammock with iron supports. Hammocks and swings, Elizabeth recalled with a slight shudder, had always made her feel seasick. A set of quoits had to be identified by Miles, but the bottles of mosquito repellent in the next package were only too familiar to them all. Four lawn chairs and half a dozen games to be played on lapboards completed the collection.

"I get the message," Reade grunted, as he gathered up the debris tidily. "The family that vacations together stays at home together—right?"

It was a little—er—oppressive, Miles admitted reluctantly. Still, the year was five months gone and, well, there was nothing to do but stick it out. Though he had begun to wonder if he had been quite sane in agreeing to test Miss Mary's theories.

They were all nuts, Reade assured him cheerfully, and how about a game of croquet?

The long twilight enabled them to see well enough for one game, the children providing an enthusiastic gallery. Afterward the two men carried the rest of what Reade called "the equipment" to the cellar, promising to put everything together the next day. They had just settled down to enjoy their evening papers when a loud shriek shattered the silence. A feminine voice began calling, "Help! Help! Police!"

Reade and Miles, followed by Grandma Lane and Elizabeth, dashed for the front door. Grandpa Lane was trapped by the children on one of the upper floors—he could be heard expostulating that he didn't know what had happened and if they would only get out of his way—

Reade and Miles were bending over something on the ground when Elizabeth turned the flashlight she had snatched from the hall table on the terrified face of a woman.

"Why, it's Mrs. Kohler!" The light provided the identification.

"You're damn right it's me!" The woman, helped to her feet, glared impartially at her rescuers. "It's no thanks to you that I haven't broken my neck. I'll report you, that's what I'll do."

To Miles's temperate rejoinder that she was trespassing, Mrs. Kohler merely sniffed. She had been in the habit of crossing this yard every night for years, and no one was going to call *that* trespassing.

She had caught her foot in a wicket and been thrown heavily to the ground, but apparently her considerable avoirdupois had cushioned her fall. She lived a block or two away, and Elizabeth Hubbard knew her only as one of the casual supermarket acquaintances she met infrequently.

147

Elizabeth and Grandma Lane managed to soothe her, and Reade courteously walked with her to the bus stop, her avowed destination.

On his return he startled the living-room group with the disclosure that Mrs. Kohler demanded that the croquet wickets be pulled up each night.

"She's ready to take it up with the City Council," he reported.

The woman was nuts, Jane and Ronnie declared. "Simply because she fell over a wicket in a place where she had no right to be—" Jane was indignant.

Ronnie said he supposed she would object if the hammock or the swing was left out overnight. It was too bad Mrs. What's-her-name hadn't broken her neck.

The next night the twins managed to leave the house unobserved—no mean feat in itself, Jane told her mother a few hours later—and were next to be seen, had anyone been curious, in Mrs. Kohler's back yard. It was not an attractive place and seemed to be used principally as a dumping space for garbage and litter. Four ancient poles loosely connected by frayed clothesline were the only ornaments.

The house had a slatternly, slouching look, and the windows that faced the yard were dark. Ronnie thought this indicated an empty house, but Jane said that probably the rooms were cooler if no lights were turned on. "Do your stuff and we'll soon find out," she urged him.

Thus encouraged, Ronnie began to bellow. "Help! Help! Police!" he yelled. "Hel-up!"

Almost instantly a light when on in a room that Jane judged to be the kitchen. A voice she identified as that of Mrs. Kohler called through the screened window.

"What's the matter out there? You take yourself off or I'll police you!"

A screen door slammed, and as a large figure charged down the back steps Ronnie dropped to the ground.

"What's the matter? What you doing here?" Mrs. Kohler clutched at Jane, who eluded her grasp.

"Your clothesline—it's nearly killed him!" Jane cried. She bent over Ronnie, who moaned.

Mrs. Kohler retreated a step. "What's the matter with him?"

"He ran into your clothesline and it nearly killed him." Jane's anguished voice was convincing. "You shouldn't keep a clothesline up at night."

"My God, you crazy or something?" The big woman tried to peer into Jane's shadowed face. "This is my own yard—you got no right to come here and tell me what I can't do."

Ronnie leaped lightly and, he hoped, dramatically to his feet.

"We have as much right to come into your yard as you have to come into ours," he announced firmly. "Ask the police, ask anyone."

"My God!" Mrs. Kohler's vocabulary was limited. "You live over on Wisteria Street. Your mother's a real nice woman," she said unexpectedly. "I'll bet she didn't send you."

The visit was their own idea, the twins admitted. And suddenly Ronnie put out his hand and smiled his perfectly charming smile.

"Let's call it quits?" he suggested.

Mrs. Kohler put her hand in his hesitantly.

"No hard feelings?" he asked. "Everything okay?"

"Okay." Mrs. Kohler smiled faintly. "You pull the wires up?"

They couldn't pull the wickets up every night, Ronnie and Jane said. Jane tried to explain the game of croquet, but although Mrs. Kohler listened intently it was clear that she did not understand. Something she mumbled convinced Jane that the poor woman thought wire wickets were to be standard equipment for all lawns and yards that summer.

"If you just walk *past* our house you'll be all right," Jane assured her. "Yes, we'll stay out of your yard, too."

By the time the twins reached home their absence had been noted, and explanations were in order. They had interrupted an argument (fortunately, they told each other, since in a measure it deflected attention from their excursion) concerning the advisability of leaving the hammock and swing outside overnight. Miles Hubbard and Reade Coleman were in favor, Grandma Lane and Elizabeth Hubbard opposed, with Grandpa Lane and Victoria May neutral. As long as he wasn't expected to tote the stuff in and out, Grandpa Lane said, he could see both sides of the question. Victoria said that she had no opinion and immediately explained that she hoped it would be remembered that there were such things as fire laws. If the front hall were to be blocked up every night with swings and hammocks, she for one would feel it her duty to report the situation to the nearest firehouse.

"I don't really feel that there is much danger of anything being taken overnight," Elizabeth admitted, "but it could happen. All these things are brand-new and might offer a temptation."

Jane's suggestion that she and Ronnie sleep outdoors was instantly vetoed. It was finally decided to gamble on the chance that (a) all the neighbors were honest and (b) most of the recreation equipment was too heavy to be easily carried away.

The night was warm and humid, and Grandpa Lane, whom nothing had ever cured of a propensity to wander around after midnight, wherever he happened to be, awoke with the intention of seeking fresh air firmly implanted in his brain. Practice had perfected his technique of getting out of bed without disturbing his wife. He put on his slippers, while trying to visualize how large a slice of the banana cream pie he dared to eat without its loss being detected. Simply from habit, he glanced out the bedroom window. Did he imagine it, or had something moved on the lawn?

His fingers trembled as he tied on his bathrobe, but his mind was busy with the puzzle of what to select as a weapon. Surprise, he had read somewhere, was nine-tenths of success in dealing with thieves, and if he could only take the—the—miscreants unawares . . . By this time he had reached the first floor, and the umbrella stand suggested the solution.

Armed with a furled umbrella, he stepped confidently out into the night—only to fall over a bundle on the lowest step of the porch. This proved to be two pillows tied together, and it cushioned what could have been a nasty fall.

"Where did you come from?" Miles Hubbard was helping him to his feet. "Lucky you didn't break your neck!"

Shaken but not abashed, Grandpa Lane snorted. Couldn't a man come out for a breath of air without risking his life, he demanded.

"And, if you must know, I saw somebody over there by the hammock—most likely after the new things."

Miles laughed. From the direction of the swing someone echoed his laughter.

"That sounds like Reade Coleman," Grandpa Lane said crossly. "What's he doing out of bed at this hour?"

He and Reade had had the same idea—to protect the castle—Miles explained, to the old man's bewilderment. Like him, they had seen "something" and had come out to ward off the foe.

Grandpa Lane regarded both men—Reade, fully dressed, had stepped out of the swing—with frank suspicion.

"You can't fool me. There's somebody in the hammock," he said.

There certainly was, Miles agreed. "My only son and heir."

Ronnie rolled out of the hammock and blinked sleepily at his audience. He wore pajamas and was barefoot.

"A lot of thanks I get for trying to protect this place from sneak thieves," he complained. "Some morning you'll wake up and find everything gone."

The fact that Ronnie had been sleeping soundly when his father investigated the hammock and that Reade had sat smoking in the lawn swing for half an hour before that made little impression on him. No one could have made off with anything without awakening him. He was a light sleeper, he declared, but his statement was rather weakened by a prodigious yawn.

Not until they were all in the kitchen raiding the refrigerator for sandwich fillings did it occur to anyone to ask about Wednesday. As a watchdog he was not precisely a success, Reade Coleman hinted. Wednesday, Ronnie explained, felt his duty to be confined to guarding the children's rooms—he would be quick to attack if danger threatened them, but he reasoned that adults were supposed to take care of themselves.

That was the moment when Wednesday, tail wagging frantically, ears alert, and eyes bright, trotted into the kitchen to beg for his share of the sandwiches.

It was finally decided, by common consent, that if the hammock was brought in every night there was little risk that anything else would be taken. As Reade pointed out, someone in the house could be counted on to hear the arrival of a truck or moving van. First Ronnie and then Jane and after her the three children all offered to sleep in the hammock every night, but their offers were not accepted.

The nights through July proved exceptionally cool, but Jane and Ronnie, whose day-camp services terminated with the first of August, prophesied that that month would be "terrific." The twins clamored for at least two weeks at the shore before school opened, and to their mother's objections pointed out that she needed a vacation as much as they did. Let Grandma Lane and Aunt Vicky look after the children for two weeks, while the Hubbards as a family unit enjoyed peace and salt air.

"All I want," Elizabeth Hubbard declared one morning, "is to have a complete day to myself. Not to be asked to do anything or go anywhere. Not to think about the meals, not to have to listen to bickering—just one day all to myself."

She and Grandma Lane were at the breakfast table alone. Reade Coleman and Miles Hubbard had left early, in Reade's car, on one of the day trips Reade had worked out as part of his vacation schedule. The question of vacations was rapidly becoming an extremely sore point in the family—Grandma Lane had been heard to say that she supposed Miss Mary wouldn't be satisfied until they were all committed to the insane asylum in a family group.

"I know how you feel," she assured Elizabeth now. "And I've been thinking—"

Jane charged into the kitchen late that afternoon to find only Grandma Lane preparing dinner.

"Where's Mums?" the girl demanded.

Grandma Lane, shelling peas, paused. "She isn't here."

"Well, she was going to return a pair of gloves at Chaton's for me today, and they're still on the hall table. Do you suppose she went downtown and forgot them?"

Behind Jane, Miles Hubbard asked impatiently if she had seen her mother. "Reade and I rush home to be on time for dinner, and there's nobody around," he complained.

"I'm here," Grandma Lane reminded him. "And the children are going to stay overnight with the Dolsons."

"But where's— With the *Dolsons*?" Miles pushed Jane into the kitchen and followed her. "Why, they live in Shelfton!"

Shelfton, the county seat, was some fifty miles from Acton. The Dolsons, with six children of their own, had been delighted when a chance meeting at a roadside market stand had disclosed that Elsie Dolson had been an old school friend of Elizabeth's "years and years ago," to quote their astonished children. Although fervent promises to keep in touch had been exchanged, his wife had not planned a definite visit, as far as Miles knew.

The kitchen screen door opened and Grandpa Lane peered in. "Elizabeth back yet?" he inquired. "Is dinner ready yet?"

"Shut the door. You're letting flies in." Grandma Lane put the peas on the stove.

From somewhere in the house Ronnie called, "Hi, Mums," and the phone rang.

"I'll get it!" Victoria must have been expecting the call. The low murmur of her voice continued for a few moments, and then she replaced the receiver just as Reade Coleman let the front door slam behind him.

"Do you have to let it slam?" she asked coldly. "I've had a terrible headache all day. That dog Wednesday's been on your bed again, too, and I put a clean spread on it only yesterday."

"I'm sorry about your head," Reade said politely. "But if you left my room door open, you can't blame Wednesday for getting on the bed."

The dog was greeting him wildly as he spoke. Victoria mumbled something under her breath and crossed the hall to the dining room. Taking her apron from one of the buffet drawers, she began to set the table.

"Have you seen Mums?" Jane accepted the silent negative shake of Victoria's head and disappeared, to be replaced almost at once by her father.

"Do *you* know where Elizabeth is, Victoria?" Miles asked. "She isn't in the kitchen."

Even to his masculine mind that seemed to call for qualification. It was only that his wife *was* usually in the kitchen around dinnertime, he said. He had been upstairs, and she was in none of the rooms.

"I haven't seen her." Victoria straightened a fork. "She could be somewhere with the children, I suppose. Ask Grandma Lane."

Experience had taught Miles not to interrupt or to get in the way of a woman getting dinner, but he was beginning to be uneasy about the nonappearance of his wife. He was just about to put the question again and demand a definite answer when Grandma Lane called to him.

"You'll have to help me get things on the table," she said. "Victoria and I can clear up, but I want the food to get to the table while it's hot." She handed Miles a plate piled high with ears of fresh corn. "I'll tell you about Elizabeth while we eat," she promised.

Dinner was dinner in Grandma Lane's book, and she believed that, regardless of the temperature, meat and potatoes should form the basis of the day's main meal, so when it was her turn to plan the menus, old-fashioned substantial courses were to be expected. Grandpa Lane's garden supplied fresh vegetables in extremely limited quantities, but he enjoyed the appreciation volubly expressed and had appointed himself inspector to pass on the quality of all vegetables bought, while secretly agreeing with Jane, who declared that for her money "frozen stuff" was just as good if not better. Jane, her father prophesied, would someday invent a capsule that, taken three times a day, would supply all needed human nourishment. Until then, he noted, she was quite willing to eat large quantities of food prepared by any good cook.

Miles and Reade together managed to carry in the steak, baked potatoes, lima beans, and peas that, in addition to the corn, were to provide adequate nutrition for the exhausted. Not until all had been served could Grandma Lane be persuaded to speak of the missing Elizabeth.

"She'll be home tomorrow morning," the old lady informed her listeners placidly. "She needed a little rest."

No, of course Elizabeth wasn't ill, she said, still quietly. Not that she wouldn't be, if she had waited until her nervous system cracked.

"Men never seem to get it into their heads that a stitch in time saves nine. Elizabeth got to the point where she could hardly breathe—and when she's caught her breath, she'll be back. That's all."

Miles was plainly bewildered. "But why didn't she tell me? Why all this secrecy?" he demanded.

Elizabeth, Grandma Lane patiently explained, simply wanted to get away by herself for a few hours. If she had told them in advance, the sheer amount of planning to be done would have worn her out. She would have felt obliged to make sure that everyone else was taken care of, that her absence in no way added to anyone's burdens or conflicted with another's desires.

"But how do we know she is safe? Did she have any money with her?" Miles Hubbard was still in shock.

"I loaned her enough." Grandma Lane's voice was soothing. "She took a bus and was going to get off when she felt like it. No, I haven't any notion where she is—after all, she isn't Jane's age. And Jane is always talking about going to Europe by herself."

When Elizabeth returned, Grandma continued sweetly, she herself would drop out of sight for a day. Without warning.

After a moment's silence, Miles Hubbard shook his head as if he hoped to clear his mind.

"Well, she'll phone tonight," he said confidently. "She'll want to know how we are."

"No, she won't phone." Grandma Lane was also confident. "I made her promise not to."

11

September, the entire household agreed (it was the only point, Jane remarked, on which they *did* agree), arrived with startling suddenness. One day, or so it seemed to them, they were complaining of the heat and humidity and envying those neighbors who had air conditioning, and then overnight a clear, almost cold air swept in, bringing relief as well as new problems. Grandpa Lane went about closing windows and doors left open for two months; Grandma Lane put a blanket at the foot of each bed; the children clamored for sweaters; Jane and Ronnie began to talk of senior-class elections; and Elizabeth Hubbard found herself cheerfully reading the advertisements for winter coats.

The house was chilly, Victoria complained regularly at

breakfast, and as regularly the three men assured her that if she ate enough substantial food she wouldn't feel cold. Grandma Lane secretly agreed with Victoria, although neither did she consider one slice of toast and one cup of coffee an adequate breakfast.

"An egg or cereal wouldn't put much weight on her," she remarked to Elizabeth Hubbard. "She's afraid of getting fat, now that she's here all day. A little more flesh, especially around her neck, would be an improvement, if you ask me."

Since Elizabeth also had a horror of putting on weight, now that she ate three meals a day at home, she was not an especially sympathetic listener. Besides, she had begun to suspect Grandma of planning the meals to include too many of Grandpa's favorite dishes. Miles was inclined to be indifferent to food, but Reade Coleman had once or twice mentioned that lima beans served five times a week were not precisely his choice. She must be very firm, Elizabeth told herself, when it came her turn to plan the menus next week.

Heat, how much and how supplied, seemed to be more important than menus for the present. The fireplace tacitly became the responsibility of Grandpa Lane, who in turn appeared to be haunted by the conviction that a severe winter was in prospect. In an effort to conserve fuel oil, he said, it was necessary to keep the fireplace going continuously. To this end he began dragging odds and ends of wood home—dead branches first, and later discarded bits of furniture left on the city curbs for the trash pickup. Only at night would he consider permitting the fireplace fire to die down, and then only after everyone but himself had gone to bed.

"He'll set the house on fire one of these nights after we're all asleep," Miles Hubbard predicted to his wife, and Reade Coleman asserted gloomily that such a disaster might be a blessing in disguise.

This was after he had fallen over a pail of water thoughtfully placed on the stairs by Grandma Lane as a safety measure.

If September was early to start worrying about an adequate supply of snow shovels—Grandpa was skeptical of the ability of the city's sanitation force to handle the blizzards he confidently predicted—it was none too early to start thinking in terms of Christmas presents, the womenfolk declared. Grandma's knitting absorbed more of her time than ever; Elizabeth Hubbard demanded that the kitchen be left to her for the making of fruitcakes; and Victoria May, who enjoyed shopping, offered to fill their lists as well as her own. She herself always wrote her Christmas cards early, she explained, because her long messages were practically letters and she needed plenty of time. To Jane's question about the *feeling* of Christmas—"Is it rampant in September?"—she answered coldly that thought was everything and that she controlled her thoughts.

To the children Christmas remained a distant delight, but the interval was to provide the special excitement of the annual school play marking Columbus Day. Robert, Leila, and Holly had all been assigned roles, and their brief lines, together with their costumes, immediately demanded the family's attention. Reade assumed the responsibility of rehearsing the small actors, and to the general surprise revealed himself as an excellent coach. Ordinarily he paid little or no heed to the children; that he could be both patient and encouraging in drilling them astonished everybody.

"I was dragged through a school play once," he said to Miles Hubbard, perhaps feeling that some explanation was necessary. "It was pure hell, but it needn't have been."

Elizabeth Hubbard, cutting and fitting and sewing the simple costumes, felt that she almost knew the play by heart from the chatter of the children. Uncle Reade, they told her, had promised to photograph them in their costumes, and they would have the prints to show their father and mother when they returned. That they could speak so matter-of-factly about their parents' absence and return had at first puzzled Elizabeth. Not once, to her knowledge, had they been homesick or seemed to miss personal contact with either father or mother. They were, she had been forced to conclude, brought up to accept separations as normal. It was probably all very up to date, and certainly easier for those left in charge, but she couldn't help feeling that something precious had been lost on both sides. But then, perhaps she was merely an old-fashioned, emotional female.

It was Ronnie who asked the question about Christopher Columbus. There was still an hour before the children's bedtime, and he and Jane, doing homework in the alcove and at the same time enjoying the rehearsal in the living room, had applauded it as letter-perfect.

"Who's going to play Christopher Columbus?" inquired Ronnie. "He must have quite a lot to say."

A boy named Merle Edmunds had the part, Robert informed him. Merle hated the whole play, but he was tall, and the teacher wanted a tall boy for the leading role.

"He keeps saying he won't wear funny clothes," Leila explained.

"I'll tell you who's really good," Robert confided. "That's Carl Leidy. You ought to hear him!"

"All the teachers say he ought to be Columbus," Holly chimed in. (She avoided the name "Christopher" as difficult to pronounce.)

"Well, then, why isn't he?" asked Reade Coleman, who had retreated behind his newspaper.

Robert was silent, but Leila spoke thoughtfully.

"You see, it's like this," she said, her manner oddly adult. "It's his mother."

"What's the matter with his mother?" Elizabeth Hubbard demanded, and Jane laughed.

"It's only that you react so defensively to the word 'mother,'" she explained apologetically. "Never mind me—go ahead, Leila, I didn't mean to interrupt you."

Carl's mother, Leila resumed, but now eying her listeners warily, was poor. There were five other children besides Carl. Mrs. Leidy worked, Leila said somewhat vaguely, and when she came home at night she was too tired to sew.

"Anyway, Carl won't ask her, on account of the stuff for costumes costs money," Robert added.

Asked who knew about the situation, the children disclosed that "all the kids" knew but none of the teachers—Carl had threatened to kill anyone who discussed his home affairs with a "nosy teacher."

"Allowing for some slight exaggeration, I'd say he's an independent lad," Reade said approvingly. "One Christopher himself would have liked to have represent him."

What there was about Christopher Columbus that appealed to Reade Coleman she couldn't fathom, and doubted that anyone else could, Victoria May repeatedly declared.

"He's simply fascinated—and for what reason?" she demanded of everyone who would listen. "At first I thought it might be the teacher. But she's fifty if she's a day, and besides, she's married. I can't make him out. He's a mystery and there is something very odd about the whole thing."

Reade paid no attention to Victoria, but he did listen to Robert, who confided that he and the school janitor had witnessed Carl enact the entire play late one afternoon after the regular rehearsal. They had sat well back in the auditorium, and Carl, in possession of the platform stage, either had not known of their presence or had accepted them as his audience. Robert was inclined to think that Carl did this often, because, unlike the majority of the other children, he was under no pressure to report promptly at home. Yes, Robert agreed, it was likely that Uncle Reade could persuade the janitor to let him watch Carl from one of the seats at the rear of the auditorium.

Reade had been prepared to accept the children's account as more enthusiastic than accurate. But, watching the small and oddly pathetic figure on the empty platform the next afternoon, and listening to the childish and yet clear voice that never once stumbled or faltered, he was honestly amazed. The photographic type of mind (of which teachers spoke so glibly) might possibly explain the boy's ability to recite the various parts, but only a remarkably strong sense of the dramatic could account for his delivery. Christopher Columbus he must be, thought Reade, by this time more thoroughly committed to the success of the play than the teacher-director.

An advocate of the direct attack, he walked down the auditorium aisle the next afternoon and greeted the startled young actor politely.

"You're very good," he assured the boy. "The play's sure to be a success with you in it."

Carl scowled. "I'm not in it," he muttered.

"You're not? Why, I took you to be Christopher Columbus—the lead. Why aren't you in the play?"

"I don't want to be, that's why."

Reade settled himself comfortably on the edge of the platform.

"Oh, if that's all—" He shrugged his shoulders. "Everyone does things he doesn't want to do."

Carl was silent.

"You must have *some* sense of obligation," Reade said. Then, as the boy looked puzzled, he added, "You owe something to your school, you know."

Still Carl did not speak.

"As I understand it, this play is to compete in a state-wide contest. It would mean a lot to everyone—your classmates even more than the teachers—to win the banner this year." Reade paused impressively. "With you as Christopher Columbus, I feel almost sure Acton will win for the primary grades."

Carl lifted a small, defiant chin. "I don't have any costume," he said. "And—and my mother, she's too busy to sew me one."

If that was all that was bothering him he needn't give it a second thought, Reade answered, taking great care to be matter-of-fact. Mrs. Hubbard was making several of the costumes, and one more would give her no trouble. He, Reade, appreciated Carl's school spirit, and luckily he already knew his lines, so there need be no extra rehearsals. They shook hands gravely, and Reade departed hurriedly to warn Elizabeth Hubbard of the need for extra material and additional secrecy. He also notified the teacher-director and the principal, who accepted the change in cast enthusiastically. The outspoken gratitude of a jubilant Merle, Reade found slightly embarrassing, but the humorous aspects consoled him.

When, early the following week, the school play was presented to an enraptured audience, Reade made sure that the Leidy family attended en masse. He took it for granted, he said, that they would let him give them a lift in his car. After all, he pointed out, it was their Carl who had the leading role in his school's play, and the least anyone could do was to make sure that the leading man's family was there to applaud him. And, after what was unanimously agreed to be a stunning success, certainly refreshments were in order. Ice cream and cake, Reade suggested to the reluctant Mrs. Leidy, were the least that could be offered to the loyal supporters of the entire cast.

The excitement of that evening had scarcely faded when

Victoria May found herself confronted by a situation for which she was totally unprepared. Later, Jane was uncharitable enough to remark that Aunt Vicky was so hopelessly out of touch with reality that she was probably not equipped to deal with any situation less than an exact duplicate of those previously encountered in her sheltered life.

It was a Friday night, and one of the rare evenings when Victoria and Jane had the living room to themselves after dinner. A church card party had attracted the adults—even Reade, who in a weak moment had yielded to Grandma Lane's pathetic complaint that there were "never enough men." Ronnie had gone to the movies, and the children were in bed.

"Aunt Vicky," said Jane, and stopped abruptly. She had been wandering around the room in a restless manner, quite unlike her usual decisive self.

"I ought to be upstairs working on my book," Victoria said fretfully. "That's what this crazy setup has done to me—when I do have time to myself, I'm too disorganized to take advantage of it."

Jane murmured something probably meant to be sympathetic. She continued to walk around the room, stopping to stare out the windows, apparently forgetting to lower the shades as Victoria had requested.

"For pity's sake, can't you settle down?" Victoria demanded impatiently. "If you haven't any homework, at least you might read a book. Or crochet—or do something. At your age you can't be having nerves."

"That's what *you* think," Jane retorted gloomily. "I've got plenty on my mind. No one ever thinks young people have worries."

To this Victoria replied, more kindly, that in the present state of the world no one was exempt from worry. No thoughtful person, she amended.

164

"Is there anything I can do?" she offered, somewhat to her own surprise.

Touchingly grateful for this evidence of interest, Jane sat down on the big old-fashioned sofa facing the center table, where Victoria had established herself with a book of crocheting instructions. She was an indifferent needlewoman, but every year toyed with the idea of making some of her Christmas presents. The usual result was that she shopped madly to fill her list the last week before Christmas.

"You see, it's like this," Jane said, and stopped.

"What is?" Victoria asked.

Jane sighed and began again.

"You probably won't understand," she said.

"If I had the slightest idea what you are talking about, I might at least try to understand." Victoria's attention appeared to be divided between Jane and the crochet book. "I wonder if a sleeveless sweater would be too complicated," she murmured.

"You aren't even listening," Jane accused her. "Aunt Vicky, I need advice awfully."

Something in the young voice penetrated Victoria's self-absorption.

"Are you in trouble, dear?" she asked sympathetically, and was shocked by Jane's sudden hoot of laughter.

"I'm not going to have a baby, if that's what you mean," the girl said, and laughed again at the expression on the older woman's face.

"I simply do not understand your generation," Victoria sighed. "You twist the most ordinary question into something tasteless and—and cheap. What is the matter with you, anyway?"

Jane, who had curled up in one corner of the sofa, might not have been listening.

"I'm worried," she announced pensively, "about Bill."

Of course she meant Bill Hazen, she retorted, in answer to Victoria's question. He had been to the house often enough, the entire family had looked him over—it was a wonder any boy ever came to the house, she added crossly, considering the inspections he had to endure.

This complaint was a familiar one, and Victoria brushed it aside. Why, she inquired bluntly, was Jane worried about Bill Hazen?

Bill and his stepfather had had another awful fight, Jane explained. The stepfather was simply impossible, and the wonder was that Bill had not left home long ago. The reason he stayed was, of course, that he had no other place to go.

"His mother ought never to have married again," Jane declared with rather shattering finality. "But then, I don't think she's any too bright."

In her opinion, Bill Hazen himself was not conspicuous for intellect, Victoria thought, but with some effort forbore to say so. She recollected him as a broad-shouldered, red-faced youth who had a tendency to drop things and knock small objects off tables. He was not, Victoria was positive, the type to worry about anything.

"Bill's home life is pretty frightful," Jane now assured her. "He can't study in peace because he's too upset. And if his marks go any lower he'll be dropped from the basketball team."

Victoria, anxious to return to the crochet book, did not see what Jane could do to solve Bill Hazen's difficulties, and said so.

"But you see, that's just it!" Jane pulled herself erect. Her lovely eyes shone with a crusader's zeal. "He only needs a decent place to live, Aunt Vicky. And that's where I can help him."

Victoria stared. "How?" she asked.

That was what she wanted to talk about, Jane replied excitedly. She didn't expect much understanding from the rest of the family; they were too conventional, too narrow-minded.

"But you're different, you look at things differently," Jane enthusiastically assured her audience of one. "Besides, you can talk Mother over, explain things to her."

The least that any friend of Bill Hazen's could do, Jane rushed on, was to offer him a home. He would be no trouble once he moved in.

"Move in here?" Victoria, startled, almost shrieked. "This house is full to the brim now," she said in a more normal tone.

Jane was silent.

"What about Bill's family?" Victoria questioned. "They're responsible for him. And even if he and the stepfather quarrel, it isn't likely that the situation is chronic."

Jane remained silent, but her attitude was tense, rather than passive.

"Where on earth would he sleep, if he did come here?" Victoria persisted reasonably. "I doubt if Ronnie would accept a roommate."

She had already asked Ronnie, Jane disclosed. He had flatly refused to take in Bill.

"Well, then—" Victoria was anxious to return to her crochet book.

"He could sleep in my room," Jane said.

"But you—" Victoria had intended to say "But where would you sleep?" but the look Jane gave her made everything too clear.

"Jane Hubbard, are you out of your mind? I never heard such revolting nonsense. What would your mother say?" The words spilled out in an unpunctuated stream. "You must be out of your mind!" Victoria finally ran out of breath.

Jane regarded her more in sorrow than in anger. People were all alike, she mourned, no one ever *understood*.

"I didn't expect *married* people to have any sense," she mumbled unhappily. "But I did expect more of you. I've always thought you had an open mind."

Poor Victoria, sensing that she had failed to come up to expectations, was nevertheless loyal to her convictions. It was unthinkable that Jane should share her bedroom with a boy. Furthermore, she did not for one moment believe that Bill Hazen's mother would consent to such a bizarre arrangement. To say nothing of the stepfather. Did Jane want to make herself the talk of the neighborhood?

Jane said that the neighborhood could go to hell. She might have known that she would get no sympathy or help in this hidebound house.

"If to be respectable is hidebound, then I'm hidebound," Victoria snapped, her never too abundant stock of patience exhausted. "And it's lucky for you that your parents are hidebound, too. I must say that I thought better of Bill Hazen—the times he's been here, he seemed like a nice, clean-minded boy. Not that he's any too bright."

Bill Hazen was no dope, Jane retorted angrily.

"To hear you all talk, you'd think everyone in this house was a Rhodes scholar. And as for being clean-minded, no one will ever be able to say that of this family!"

Exactly what did Bill think of the idea, Victoria asked, with considerable curiosity. Was Jane acting on his suggestion?

Jane was infuriated to find herself blushing. Bill knew nothing of the proposed arrangement, she admitted. To save him possible disappointment she had intended to wait until she could definitely offer him a place to stay.

"Are you planning for him to be here for meals?" Victoria was evidently suffering a second shock. "He has a home and a family to support him. Why should he move in here?"

Jane put her head down on her knees and moaned. There was no use in discussing it further, she muttered; she might have known that no one would *understand*. It occurred to Victoria that the vocabulary of the young was limited, but heroically she refrained from mentioning it. Instead, she suggested that after a good night's sleep Jane would undoubtedly see things in a different light—failing to recognize the cliché as a favorite in the stock collection of the middle-aged.

Partly because she had promised to say nothing to Elizabeth Hubbard, a nagging anxiety kept Victoria closely observant of Jane during the next week. A direct question had revealed that Bill Hazen still knew nothing of Jane's altruistic efforts in his behalf, and he was in and out of the house much as usual. But during the second week he was, to quote Grandma Lane, "conspicuous by his absence."

"I miss him," she confided seriously, "because he was always eating something. He just about ruined my fruit-bowl centerpiece every time he came."

Jane said nothing. They had probably quarreled, Victoria assumed, and thought comfortably that it was all for the best.

"It certainly is odd, the way Bill Hazen seems to have disappeared," Grandma Lane remarked, breaking the concentrated silence of the living room one evening after the children had gone to bed.

Elizabeth, dressing a blonde doll for Holly's already large family of dolls, was not especially interested in Bill Hazen, but the mention of his name alerted Victoria. She glanced toward the alcove and saw that Jane continued to write busily.

From behind his inevitable newspaper, Miles Hubbard repeated the name. "Bill Hazen? That the broad-shouldered boy who lives on Elwood Street?"

"For heaven's sake!" Elizabeth Hubbard never ceased to be surprised by the oddments dredged up in her husband's memory. "How did you know where he lives?"

"Know his stepfather," Miles explained.

"Well, what about him?" his wife prodded, since nothing more came from behind the printed page.

"Yes, what about him, Dad?" Ronnie called, looking over Jane's bent head.

Miles put down his paper, surprised to find himself the evident center of attention.

"What about what?" he asked good-naturedly.

His wife sighed in exasperation. She said something under her breath that sounded like "Deliver me from men" and motioned to Ronnie to keep quiet. Speaking with exaggerated distinctness, she asked her husband what he knew about Bill.

"Why, when it comes down to that, nothing," Miles replied cheerfully. "Nothing at all. I remember seeing him about the house now and then—not that I ever took much notice of him. But his stepfather happened to mention him. Just in passing. He didn't say much."

"Well, what did he say?" Elizabeth demanded.

"Oh, only that they had had a postcard from Bill, saying he had arrived safely," Miles said. "Seems his mother had begun to worry."

Both Jane and Ronnie were staring at their father now. Ronnie was the first to speak. "Where'd he go?" he gulped.

His father, anxious to return to his paper, obviously decided to part with whatever information he had. Bill, according to his stepfather, had gone to Wyoming to live with a married sister. No, he had not told anyone of his plans and in effect had run away.

"But I gather that, since the sister is willing to have him, no one will take any legal steps. She must have sent him the money for his fare secretly, and he told no one and took nothing with him. It will be a relief to his mother—it can't have been pleasant for her to have her son and her husband at loggerheads."

Even if Ronnie had not ejaculated "For Pete's sake!" and Jane had not stifled another exclamation by putting her hand over her mouth, their surprise would have been evident. Their father was again absorbed in his paper, but Victoria was conscious of a tenseness in the atmosphere.

"Didn't you know?" she asked, as Jane dropped her pencil.

"Nobody knew." Ronnie looked dazed. "He never said a word, did he, Jane?"

Jane, crawling about on the floor, lifted a flushed face. "I suppose he made up his mind in a hurry," she said doubtfully. "And then, too, he wouldn't want his stepfather to know—he might have kept him from going." She got to her feet, placed the retrieved pencil carefully on the table. "His sister must be a nice girl," she said.

For a moment no one spoke, and then Grandma Lane remarked cheerfully that it seemed extravagant to buy pumpkins when they had such a fine home-grown crop. This statement instantly attracted her husband's attention, as she had hoped, and supplied a fresh topic for general conversation.

His pumpkin crop was the outstanding achievement of Grandpa Lane's gardening heart. In quality and in size it had so far exceeded his expectations that it had seemed almost irreverent to him that they should be coveted for pies. Scarcely less blasphemous he considered the children's pleas that they be transformed into lanterns.

"But what are you going to use them *for?*" his exasperated wife demanded. "They won't keep forever, you know."

Women, she was informed, always had to turn everything into something else. They had no capacity for enjoying real beauty. They couldn't look at anything with pleasure unless they could cut it or cook it or in some way put it to work. Grandpa was as much astonished by his eloquence as the other members of the family were, and a respectful silence followed his outburst.

When the twins first spoke again, it was in whispers.

The pumpkin crop was stored in the cellar, which was cool and dry, but the oil burner annoyed the gardener, who would cheerfully, or so his wife said, have been willing to see the family freeze to death if by turning off all heat he could prolong the life of his pumpkins. The children delighted Grandpa by their enthusiastic admiration of his prize crop, and almost daily they brought in school friends to see the display. Leila was overheard to say that only pumpkins that "weren't good-looking" were ever used in pies or to make lanterns.

It was Leila who stunned the breakfast table a few days later with her excited announcement that the pumpkins had been stolen.

"What do you mean, stolen?" Robert asked skeptically.

Grandpa Lane shook his head. "You can't get a rise out of me, young lady," he said genially. "No one goes about stealing pumpkins."

Leila scowled, but she kept her temper and managed to convey the impression that this attitude invoked only her pity.

"Well, they're gone," she said, and continued to eat toast.

"How do you know they're gone?" probed Jane.

Leila swallowed a bit of toast the wrong way, which might have accounted for her exasperation.

"Because they're not in the cellar, that's why," she rasped. "I went down to see this morning, and they're all gone."

Grandpa Lane looked at her with horror. He pushed back his chair, his hands shaking.

"They were there last night," he mumbled. "I saw them just before I went up to bed."

Leila, conscious of sudden unpopularity, defended her statements. She had gone down to the cellar just before breakfast to get a yellow apple, and there were no pumpkins there. No, she didn't know who had stolen them, or when, but they couldn't just walk out of the house, could they? This paraphrase of a favorite remark of Grandma Lane's caused Jane to giggle, but she apologized.

"I'll go down and look, shall I?" she offered.

Grandpa Lane was already halfway to the door that opened on the cellar stairway. He paid no attention to Miles Hubbard's direction to Ronnie to go down and look, or to Grandma's nervous admonitions not to fall. Ronnie and Jane and the three children trailed after him.

"No one would steal pumpkins," Elizabeth Hubbard said to her depleted breakfast table. "What would they want with them?"

However, the pumpkins had vanished, and it was not much consolation to discover that Grandpa Lane himself had forgotten to padlock the outside cellar door. Oddly enough it was the children's sympathy that seemed to offer him the most comfort, and he gratefully accepted their warmhearted commiseration.

A week later Miles Hubbard, whose hobby was photography, was persuaded by a fellow enthusiast to attend a showing of prize prints sponsored by a local camera club. The usual shoptalk of superb lighting effects, unique angles, and trick poses made small impression upon him, and he was prepared to write off the show as commonplace until suddenly he found himself looking at a series of prints of lighted pumpkins, ten (he counted mechanically) in all.

As a study in lighting the prints were fascinating. Whoever had carved the faces had known how to handle a knife—the exhibitor's name was strange to Miles, whose attention was riveted. A conviction that he was staring at Grandpa Lane's cherished pumpkins firmed in his mind. Pumpkins, as far as he knew, had no individual marks of identification, and proof of ownership would certainly be difficult to establish. Better not say anything to the bereaved gardener, he told himself, until he could be sure. The photographs, according to the card attached, had been entered in a national contest. He might, Miles decided, call up the photographer and congratulate him—any good cameraman would consider that the perfect introduction.

It was a pity, he grumbled to himself, that a phone booth could not be installed in the house—the lack of privacy was positively indecent at times. If he made the call before going home he would probably be late for dinner and that would worry his wife. After nearly twenty-five years of marriage she still thought the slightest change in his time schedule predicted disaster. He really should have asserted himself years ago, he thought, and decided to use the phone booth in the lobby, after all.

A young, pleasant, masculine voice answered his call. Yes, he was Howard Hill, and, yes, he had several prints entered in the current exhibition of the Trant Camera Club. He forbore to ask "Why?" although obviously he was puzzled.

The prints of the pumpkins had especially interested him, Miles said smoothly. He touched briefly on the technicalities of lighting and shading, warmly congratulating the exhibitor on his artistic success. He added that the subject matter had struck him as unusual in a city show. Had Mr. Hill had any special—er—memories associated with—er—with pumpkins?

"Never gave 'em two thoughts," the obviously young Mr. Hill answered cheerfully. "I just happened to see these on a produce stand a couple of blocks down the street. My photographs, by the way, are usually more or less experimental. I'm not a professional."

He was damn good, Miles assured him sincerely, and added, casually, that he'd been looking for large pumpkins to be carved into lanterns for his young children.

"Well, the guy might have some left." Mr. Hill sounded

doubtful. "Anyway, no harm in trying. The name's Londa, J. B. Londa, and he's on the left-hand side of Halsey Street."

Miles thanked him and hung up. Now he would surely be late for dinner, but all his life he had prided himself on finishing whatever he began. Grandpa Lane's pumpkins had become a matter of principle with him, and he was committed to following any lead, however tenuous.

J. B. Londa's shop was small, crowded, and not very clean. A dejected-looking woman who had all too obviously given up the attempt to dye her gray hair black sat on a box outside, under the tattered awning. The only light in the store was a single unshaded bulb that dangled above the cash register.

She replied to Miles's polite query for pumpkins with one word, "No." He thought she seemed dazed, rather than hostile, and he waited a moment before he asked if he might speak to Mr. Londa.

This time she looked definitely frightened. "You from the police?" she asked, and added, "Again?"

He had nothing to do with the police, Miles assured her impatiently. All he wanted of Mr. Londa was to ask where he had bought some pumpkins and where—

To his dismay the woman began to cry, slow painful tears, which she attempted to dry with her dirty apron. She was mumbling "Go away! Go away!" when a younger woman appeared from somewhere back in the shop.

"I'm looking for Mr. Londa," Miles said.

"He isn't here."

"Well, can you tell me anything about some pumpkins?" Miles tried not to sound impatient.

The older woman was crying noisily now. All he wanted, Miles explained, was to know where Mr. Londa got the pumpkins that he had sold to an artist, who had photographed them.

175

"I've got nothing to do with the police. And if I could speak with Mr. Londa for just a minute—"

"Well, if you must know—" the younger woman shrugged in resignation—"he's probably in jail. At least he went away with the cops. They said a gang of boys stole the pumpkins and sold them to Mr. Londa. Could he help that?"

Miles thought it probable that Mr. Londa had had previous dealings with unreliable suppliers of produce, but there was no further reason to pursue his investigation. He was already late for dinner, and the news he had obtained would contribute nothing to cheerful family table conversation. For some inexplicable reason he felt he should buy something—the women in Mr. Londa's family were certainly a depressed-looking pair. He settled for half a dozen handsome apples, and for the remainder of the short walk home wondered uneasily if he might not have involved himself in an illegitimate transaction.

Grandpa Lane continued to mourn his loss, but sided with the children, who refused to hold Wednesday in any part to blame. How could a watchdog get out of the house, Grandpa demanded, with all the doors locked at night? As for the daytime, no self-respecting dog would be looking for thieves in broad daylight. People were supposed to look after themselves during the day. Next year, if he lived, he intended to have the garden equipped with an electric alarm.

Part Three

Melinda Drew

12

Thanksgiving, Miss Mary Hall instructed me, was the really true family holiday.

"I think each member of our family circle should be allowed to ask two guests, Melinda," she said to me early in November. "That will add to their sense of belonging, don't you think?"

I said that I thought thirty-three people were more than could be comfortably seated or fed anywhere except in a hotel.

"But perhaps you're not thinking of the three children?" I suggested hopefully. "I don't think it matters much either way to them."

Well, it should matter, Miss Mary retorted with some asperity. The way to instill hospitable instincts in children was to begin early. She thought it important to train the children to welcome guests and to be responsible for their pleasure and comfort.

As diplomatically as possible, I argued that crowding thirty-three people in an ordinary-sized dining room would definitely interfere with the pleasure and comfort of all.

"What about a second table for the children?" Miss Mary proposed. "I remember, when I was a child and we went to my grandmother's house for holiday dinners, the children ate after the grownups had finished. We didn't have leftovers, or anything like that," she assured me. "It was the same dinner as the adults, only an hour or so later."

There were usually at least a dozen children at these affairs, she admitted, when I asked her. She recalled several years when there had been as many as twenty.

"I'm not sure it would work today," she confessed, perhaps sensing my lack of enthusiasm. "I mentioned it to a grand-niece of mine last year, and she had a fit. Said that in her opinion children should be served first and the adults have the second table. Times do change so."

I didn't think a second table for children was a good solution of our difficulties, I said. It might be better to have the children seated at their own little table (from which they could be supervised) and to limit the guest invitations to the grownups. I didn't think the children would care, and, in fact, it might be difficult to find any children among their friends who would be free to come if asked. Thanksgiving, I reminded Miss Mary, was a family holiday.

So it was finally decided that I suggest to Miss Mary's "family" that each of them invite two guests to Thanksgiving dinner. Some slight confusion resulted immediately—and should have warned me of what the future held in store—by the

Lanes' supposition that they were *each* entitled to have two guests. Elizabeth Hubbard was, as usual, sensible about the ensuing argument and finally succeeded in convincing the old people that, since she and her husband were together having only two guests, the Lanes should be willing to conform.

I was rather curious about what the twins would do, or say, and not too surprisingly Jane asked two boys and Ronnie invited two girls. Their families, Jane informed me when I displayed some curiosity, always ate Thanksgiving dinner in a large hotel and were rather pleased to be relieved of the responsibility for teen-age guests. Times, to quote Miss Mary, do change.

I had been prepared for some bickering about the menu, but it was comparatively slight. What did cause "ructions," to quote Grandma Lane, was the question of when dinner should be served. Grandma Lane and Elizabeth Hubbard stoutly declared that four o'clock was the traditional hour in their homes and, to hear them tell it, in the majority of homes in which English was spoken.

The menfolk—Grandpa Lane, Miles Hubbard, and Reade Coleman—held out for six o'clock, after the TV football games. Victoria thought two in the afternoon was "correct," and the twins insisted that eight o'clock was "classy," an idea their mother told me they had picked up from seeing English movies.

Eventually, five o'clock was the compromise reached, with cocktails at four.

"Grandma thinks we're going to hell, of course," Jane told me. "But her good manners won't let her rise up and warn the company of the evil of their ways. She'll have about two gallons of tomato juice prominently displayed. Do you want to bet that Grandpa doesn't get away with more than one well-diluted Martini?"

I said I didn't want to bet.

"What Ronnie and I would really like to do," Jane declared pensively, "would be to go to the movies—the six of us, I mean. Only we haven't enough money."

She refused my offer of a loan rather indignantly. I wasn't to think she had been hinting, and anyway, there were no good movies at the neighborhood theaters that week.

As it happened, a heavy snowfall solved the teens' problem of what to do with themselves before the company arrived. A light snow began Thanksgiving Eve and steadily increased throughout the night. It stopped shortly after seven the next morning, leaving impressive drifts that offered alarming threats of permanence.

It was Victoria May who telephoned me the information that Jane and Ronnie were "shoveling like mad" and were planning to reap a fortune by clearing steps and sidewalks for less active Acton residents.

"And, if you'll forgive the lateness of the invitation, will you be my guest for Thanksgiving dinner?" she asked calmly.

My first impulse was to decline—evidently someone had let her down, and it was scarcely flattering to be asked to fill in, and as late as this. On the other hand, Marge Carter, with whom I had been pledged to dine, had been stricken by flu; I was frankly curious to see Miss Mary's family in a normal situation; and, finally, my ego had been permanently flattened for years. As Jane might have said, what did I have to lose?

"I'd love to come, Miss May," I warbled brightly, and the moment she hung up I returned peacefully to bed. Holiday-morning sleep is precious to the laborer, and for the past week I had been serving as temporary private secretary to an irascible old gentleman whose chief occupation, at eighty-three, was to add to his famous collection of stamps. I had been told that his permanent secretary found it necessary to take time off at regular intervals to preserve her sanity, and I believed it. It did occur to me now, just before I lost consciousness, to question my own sanity. Why in the world had I let myself get tangled up with Miss Mary's experiment on one of the few days I might have reasonably called my own?

I could not have been asleep more than twenty minutes when the phone rang again. And again it was Victoria. Why couldn't the woman work on her book instead of calling up weary people who needed all the sleep they could get? A holiday should give her the extra time she was always coveting, and here she was wasting it making unnecessary phone calls. Too late, I reminded myself that I could have left the receiver off the hook.

"I thought I'd better prepare you, Mrs. Drew," Victoria said.

She stopped abruptly. Naturally, I asked, "Prepare me for what?" and tactfully suppressed a yawn.

"Well, it's like this." Victoria's tone suggested that she was comfortably settled and ready for a nice, long chat.

It was therefore slightly startling to have her begin to whisper.

"There may not be any Thanksgiving dinner—I thought I'd better tell you," she murmured, managing to sound conspiratorial. "Although it isn't certain yet," she added.

I probably said something like "Why not?" for she continued, her voice sounding a little clearer as she went on. The trouble stemmed, she informed me, from fiction in the kitchen. "I mean friction," she corrected herself hastily.

I said I didn't understand, which was an understatement. "Friction in the kitchen" might mean almost anything.

"It's like this," Victoria explained. "There are three turkeys to be stuffed—three ought to be enough, don't you think?"

Depending on the size, I admitted cautiously, three turkeys

might supply enough meat and dressing to be more than enough for a good-sized family. To which Victoria replied that the dressing was the trouble.

She seemed determined to keep me asking "Why?" Rather meanly, I kept silent.

"Grandma Lane insists on putting sage in the stuffing," Victoria said after a long pause. "Her mother always put sage in the stuffing. It's Grandpa Lane who argued about it after they were married."

I weakened and asked what was the matter with sage, to be told that the Hubbards violently disliked the flavor. Since I am no lover of sage myself, I secretly sympathized with the Hubbards, but I did not feel that, as a prospective guest, I should do any dictating.

"You're probably thinking that Pauline and Christy can bake a small pan of dressing without sage in it," Victoria said. "But that wouldn't settle anything."

Pauline and Christy were the two young, competent, trained cooks I had supplied from Miss Mary's pet agency. They were to be supplemented by two waitresses at dinnertime.

My sympathies were with Pauline and Christy. I didn't see why a separate pan of stuffing without sage wouldn't be a good solution of the problem, and said so.

"Well, for one thing, Grandpa Lane insists that the only 'decent' turkey stuffing is an oyster dressing." The contempt in Victoria's tone was withering.

"How many, besides Grandpa Lane, like oyster dressing?" I asked.

He was the only one who could abide it, Victoria testified disdainfully. For herself, give her good, sensible stuffing, with a touch of thyme, perhaps, but not too much.

"Jane thinks chopped almonds would be good," she added.

"But Jane puts chopped almonds in everything she eats—she's no cook."

I abandoned all hope of being allowed to resume my sleep. Let one turkey have the sage stuffing, I decreed, one oyster stuffing, and the third a stuffing made from the "neutral," traditional recipe, if there was one.

"No one eats much dressing, anyway," I instructed Victoria. "And usually it's ignored completely once dinner is over."

I was ready to hang up, with that problem solved, but Victoria had other troubles to impart.

"The girls"—I suppose she meant Pauline and Christy—"had to make two kinds of cranberry sauce, and they said it was a nuisance. I've always thought there was only one way to make cranberry sauce—clear, like jelly. But Grandma Lane insisted the berries must be left in, so we'll be having both."

I didn't understand why Victoria should be so deeply interested in the Thanksgiving dinner details; hitherto she had never, as far as I knew, bothered about menus or food. And then, almost as if she had read my mind, she offered the explanation.

"My friend Sarah Hauser is very knowledgeable about food," she told me. "She writes recipes for a syndicate. And since she's to be one of my guests, naturally I'd like to have everything just right."

What Grandma Lane and Elizabeth Hubbard thought or would think of this situation was a question I preferred not to examine.

"There's just one thing more," Victoria said hurriedly. "It's about the dessert."

Of course there would be mince and pumpkin pies, she impatiently answered my murmured reminder, but Grandpa Lane wasn't satisfied with pie as a dessert.

"He wants something called Indian pudding—it has to be

boiled first and then baked, he says, and served hot with ice cream. The children heard about the ice cream, and now nothing will satisfy them but Indian pudding. Neither Pauline nor Christy has ever heard of it. Have you?"

I'd heard of it, I admitted, but never tasted it. I had an idea it was made of corn meal, and boiled first in a cloth. Certainly Pauline and Christy couldn't be bothered to make it now. If Grandpa Lane's nostalgic reminiscences continued past Thanksgiving, I'd hunt up a recipe and he could have his Indian pudding later.

I had dressed and was eating breakfast before the phone rang again. This time it was Christy, and from her first word I knew that she was beginning to realize that she was in no ordinary household.

"It's the maraschino cherries, Mrs. Drew," she said. "They're gone. And I need them to top the grapefruit."

A first course of grapefruit untopped by a cherry was not to be thought of, I agreed. But, I suggested tentatively, I had ordered two large jars, hadn't I?

"Both of them—he took both of them." Christy sounded grim. "Any ordinary old gentleman would be dead, eating two jars of maraschino cherries, but Mr. Lane is tough. Nothing kills him. At least," she added as an afterthought, "I haven't found his body anywhere yet."

To my rather feeble remonstrance that no one would eat two jars of maraschino cherries, she said, with a kind of gloomy relish, that I didn't know Grandpa Lane. If she and Pauline hadn't watched him every minute of the day before— when the advance preparations got under way—there would not have been a nut or a raisin or a piece of citron left in the house.

"At his age, you'd think it would kill him," Christy observed, with the cheerful indifference of the young.

I had promised Elizabeth Hubbard to be at the house by two

o'clock. There wasn't anything I could do, she had assured me, but my presence had a good effect on her nerves! This statement, meant to be complimentary, I'm sure, tended to make *me* nervous. Not that I actually expected to walk in on a heated argument the instant Reade Coleman opened the door for me, but perhaps I should have been prepared.

The difficulty, as Elizabeth Hubbard delicately labeled the dispute, centered on the serving of sherry. Miss Mary had sent two dozen bottles of imported sherry, and it was in the pantry ready to be served by the attractive young waitresses I stumbled over in the hall.

"They're having a fight," one of them whispered to me. "The old lady, she says she won't have any drunken revelers in her house."

"And Miss Victoria, she says it isn't her house." The other girl, rather obviously enjoying the excitement, whispered, too.

"What I'd like to know—" the first girl spoke briskly—"is whose house is it?"

I hung up my coat and took off my storm boots without attempting to answer. The first thing to be done was to try to establish peace in the living room before time for the guests to arrive.

"Hello!" I said, as brightly as I could, from the doorway. "Do you know you have the cleanest pavement and steps of any house I've so far seen?"

Ronnie and Jane beamed, but no one else even smiled. Grandma Lane's face was flushed, and Grandpa was patting her arm and murmuring "Now, now," without any visible effect.

"There's no reason why we can't serve tomato juice or fruit cocktails," Elizabeth Hubbard said, evidently too engrossed with her subject to be interrupted. "But guests should certainly be offered a choice. No one is going to get intoxicated on sherry."

I could have predicted Grandma Lane's reply, and she didn't let me down.

"It's a matter of principle," she asserted. "I shall never approve of liquor being served in the home. Think of the children—"

Reade Coleman seized the opportunity with unconcealed delight.

"Following that reasoning," he said, his rich, deep voice deliberately unhurried, "coffee should not be served in a house where children live. Going still further, perhaps we should ban certain *foods* that are considered unsuitable in children's diets. How do you feel about that, Ronnie?"

Ronnie grinned amiably and remarked that he couldn't care less.

"Dad takes the underage laws seriously," he explained, with the tolerance of youth for the foibles of age—you would have thought his father to be approaching ninety at least.

"What Ronnie really means," Jane said kindly, "is that he thinks the stuff is overrated. So do I. I'd rather have Coke any day in the week."

I silently awarded Miles Hubbard a gold star for tactful child training. The years of work were certainly beginning to pay off.

Eventually the sherry argument was settled. The solution was so simple and so obvious that I wondered if there might not be other mounting tensions within the family circle to account for the personal animosities that seemed to develop with each sign of discord.

Grandma Lane was given the responsibility for the soft drinks and Reade Coleman placed in charge of the sherry. He thought there should be a wider choice, but Victoria reminded him that no one was giving a cocktail party and that, on Thanksgiving, dinner was the attraction. After that everyone disappeared to dress, leaving the two waitresses—Kit and Kat,

188

they called themselves, and confided that eventually they hoped to be on the stage—to exchange notes with Pauline and Christy while they set out the glasses.

It showed the state of my nerves when Grandma Lane, the first to be dressed and downstairs, cornered me to make the announcement that she knew I had been worried and so had "taken steps" to put my mind at ease. I am sure I turned pale, but I had put on rouge. Anyway, Grandma wanted only a listener, and unless I fell on the floor in a faint she wasn't likely to be alarmed.

"I knew you were worried about the turkey stuffings," she hissed, glancing over her shoulder as if I were her partner in an intrigue. "The turkey on the big blue plate has the sage stuffing, the one on the green platter has oyster stuffing, and the bird still in its pan has the regular old-style dressing, with lots of chopped onion—I saw to that. There was plenty for gravy in the two pans."

She was so manifestly pleased with herself, so certain that she had relieved my anxiety, that I could only thank her and praise her ingenuity. Before her black satin and white-ruffled "best" gown had disappeared through the doorway and into the hall, I had forgotten the significance of the colored plates—not, it developed, that this mattered.

The most delicious odors permeated the house by the time the first guests arrived. A blazing fire crackled in the living-room fireplace, and the dropping outside temperature accented the glow of hospitality. I was gazing happily upon the festive scene and congratulating myself that this was to be one occasion on which nothing went wrong when Christy, coming up behind me and whispering, "If you please, ma'am," startled me.

"It's the plates," she said, still in a whisper.

The doorbell rang blithely and another contingent of guests arrived. In the flurry of getting them unwrapped and sorted out, Christy steered me into the pantry. She was breathing heavily and looked a portent of disaster if I ever saw one.

"It's the turkeys, ma'am," she groaned, this time confirming my fears.

"Don't tell me—they're burned to a crisp and we'll have to have omelets," I said. "Do we have enough eggs?"

There was nothing wrong with the turkeys, she assured me. It was the plates. Didn't I remember the plates?

"Blue and green so we can tell 'em apart," she reminded me.

The scheme for distinguishing the different dressings returned to my memory. But what was wrong with the plates?

"It was Kit," Christy explained, not too coherently. "She saw the blue plate and she thought it was too valuable—'a heirloom,' she calls it. So she takes it on herself to get another, and because she finds two big, plain white plates in the kitchen cupboard she slips the turkeys off on them and washes up the colored plates. 'You never know when accidents can happen,' she says to me."

Of course, any girl with half a brain should have known that two cooks as experienced as herself and Pauline didn't break dishes, Christy continued. But kids these days—

I interrupted her monologue on the failings of modern youth (I knew it by heart) to ask again what was wrong with the plates.

"Kit didn't pay any attention to the turkeys!" Christy wailed, her voice rising. "She shuffled 'em, you might say. And now who's to tell where the oyster stuffing is, let alone the sage?"

I thought it only reasonable to conclude that the stuffings were in the turkeys, but Christy's anxiety was real, and I tried to be sympathetic. Kit had been horrified, I learned, when her error had been explained to her, and was now being alternately lectured by Pauline and comforted with hot tea.

"If worst comes to worst, you can always taste a bit of the

dressing before serving it," I suggested brightly. "Luckily you don't have to worry about your figure, Christy."

Christy, the bean-pole type, was too worried to smile. The perfectionist leads a hard life.

I could only advise her to "think positive," a favorite expression of one of my old uncles, and in the cheerful predinner conversation and the bustle of welcoming guests I forgot the subject. Because of the difference in seasonings—never again, I promised myself that night, would I be party to such an idiotic arrangement—the turkeys were carved in the pantry. Each guest was asked his preference, and the first thing that went wrong was that Grandpa Lane, scarlet-faced, was seething with indignation. Across the table from me, Victoria was muttering—I caught the words "incompetent . . . incredible"—and then Leila spoke distinctly.

"It tastes funny!" she said.

The three children had a small table to themselves, and Jane had volunteered to keep an eye on them. I had overheard her drilling them in table etiquette an hour ago, and she looked dismayed.

"If you don't like it, don't eat it," she told them fiercely. "You don't have to make any remarks."

I looked around the dining room, and it seemed to me that most of the carefully made stuffings were being left untouched on the diners' plates. Stories of mass food poisonings began to stir in my mind. How dreadful if this dinner, on which Miss Mary had lavished so much thought and for which she had provided truly beautiful extra silver and glassware and exquisite linens, should prove a near tragedy. That something was wrong was evident, but what had happened? Then, with a suddenness that was unnerving, I recollected the plates!

Under other circumstances, I think I would have remained silent, but here the family was forced to accept a situation for which it was not responsible. Why not simply explain? Kit's name need not be mentioned, and perhaps the sense of all sharing in a mild version of a hostess's nightmare might dissolve the stiffness that so far not even the sherry had been able to erase.

My intuition proved correct, and after my explanation the atmosphere did relax. Nearly everyone had a story to tell of an embarrassing domestic experience, and by the time the dessert course was reached it was evident that "the party," as the children called it, was a success. It was the children who provided the only discordant note.

Their dessert was to be pumpkin pie topped with ice cream, and they were to have hot cocoa as a substitute for coffee—it was important, Jane had instructed everyone who would listen, that their menu conform as closely as possible to that enjoyed by the adults.

"Children need to relate," Jane had told her somewhat dazed mother, who later confided to me that she was sick of the word "relate."

Robert waited until he and his sisters had been served their pie and ice cream. Then, when Kit put his portion down before him, he pushed it aside.

"I want Indian pudding," he said loudly.

Kit was tired and in no mood to conciliate an irritating small boy. There was no Indian pudding, she told him.

Leila and Holly instantly demanded to know where "the Indian" was and to Kit's bewildered "What Indian?" insisted that she produce the "pudding Indian."

Some fifteen minutes later—after Leila and Holly had wept and lamented confusedly and Robert had been ordered by Miles Hubbard to apologize to Kit (he had accused her of killing the Indian)—the misunderstanding had been straightened out. All three children had associated Indian pudding with the American Indian and had expected some souvenir, or perhaps a tribal trademark (Robert had hoped for a bow and arrow), to accompany the pudding. Even after the crushing announcement that there would be no Indian pudding, the youngsters had comforted themselves with the hope that they might at least be vouchsafed a sign, if only a single feather.

Exhausted by grief and much food, they were in no condition to protest an early curfew, and the adults, in a comfortably lethargic state themselves, settled in the living room for what Grandma Lane described as "the lost art of conversation." I had hoped to get away early, but first Reade Coleman tackled me on the subject of Miss Mary's opinion of her experiment—did she feel she was proving anything?—and then Sarah Hauser, the food expert, lectured me a bit on the subject of proper diets for the aging. I was inching my way toward the hall, with the intention of making an unobtrusive exit, when an elderly woman—I'd forgotten her name, although I remembered she was Grandma Lane's guest—caught my arm.

"Just a minute, Mrs. Drew. You are Mrs. Drew, aren't you? I won't keep you a minute—I only want to ask you one question."

She had very pretty gray hair and wore a gray silk dress trimmed with jet. Her eyes were like small jet buttons.

"I thought it could do no harm to ask you—I believe in looking ahead." The jet-button eyes stared unwinkingly into mine. "Myrtle Lane invited me here for dinner today, and I thought I'd ask you, if anything should happen to her—if she should die or anything—could I have her place here? I mean move in—I understand the requirements are kind of special."

13

Holidays seemed to stimulate Miss Mary. The day after Thanksgiving she phoned me from her office—she had given her secretary the weekend off—to ask me to meet with her there at ten o'clock. We ought to discuss, she said, with her customary energy, an idea on which she needed my advice. A tactful woman, Miss Mary Hall! And not one to waste words.

"I have long felt that the observance of Christmas has become too commercial," she said, the instant I was seated in the chair beside her desk. "And I've decided to do something about it."

She had a plan fairly well worked out in her mind, she told me, but must depend on me to put it into action. The familiar feeling of nervousness I had come to associate with Miss

Mary's projects rang a warning bell, but my curiosity was stronger.

"What have you decided?" (I have never been one to count ten.)

"Well, really, it's very simple." Miss Mary beamed happily. "I haven't thought it out completely yet, but you'll know how best to handle it. My idea is that the family should set an example."

She looked expectantly at me, but the best I could do was to repeat, idiotically, "An example?"

"Yes, you know what I mean. It's all very well to voice criticism, but action speaks louder than words." She might have been addressing the Acton Women's Club.

But my bewilderment finally made an impression, and she began to explain. Her plan was to get the family to agree to buy no gifts for relatives and friends, giving instead their talents and time. She wouldn't rule out what she called "homemade" gifts, Miss Mary said—her idea was to preserve the spirit of Christmas, and handwork certainly represented the giver's talent and time. It would all work out smoothly, she assured me brightly. She regretted that she had not thought of the plan earlier, but it had occurred to her only the night before, when she could not sleep.

The accent was, of course, to be on giving, she insisted, but gifts were to cost the giver personal effort rather than money. When I reflected on the expenditure of personal effort usually demanded of the Christmas shopper, my inclination was to laugh. Long gift lists and short bank balances were a part of the commercial observance of Christmas, perhaps, but the resultant poverty certainly cost personal effort, if that was what Miss Mary valued most.

The discussion ended with my promise to present the suggestion to the family that night. In a way, it was a relief to have something on which to build a conversation—from Elizabeth Hubbard I had learned that the living-room evenings were becoming increasingly dull. No one had anything to talk about, she had said, and friction usually developed when there *was* any conversation.

"We all get on each other's nerves, I guess," she concluded unhappily. "And yet it's strange, when by this time we all know each other so well."

I asked her to try to have the group assembled after dinner that night, whereupon she surprised me by saying that it would be better if I made Grandma Lane my spokesman.

"She's always saying that she is ignored and that she and Grandpa ought to be considered the heads of the family." Elizabeth sounded a little grim. "I try to remember it's her age, but I do get worn out with trying not to hurt her feelings."

Grandma's feelings were not the only ones ruffled, I decided that evening when Jane ushered me into the living room. The chess game had been interrupted, and Miles Hubbard and Reade Coleman had evidently found the evening papers a poor substitute. Grandpa Lane sat in a corner, removed as far as possible from the television set, which Victoria May had to herself—it must have been her night to view one of the series. Ronnie surveyed me from the alcove, and only Grandma Lane, placidly knitting under one of the side lights, appeared relaxed. The three children were in bed and, I hoped, asleep.

The warmth of my welcome could have been variously interpreted, but I chose to assume they were glad to see me. I came from Miss Mary, I said frankly, and had something to tell them that would be of interest to them all. Jane had pulled a chair up to the round table, and as I seated myself they insensibly began to close in to form a ragged circle under the center light.

The house was deliciously warm, and something of the holiday atmosphere lingered in the air. Grandma Lane was wearing her best black dress with the white ruffles, and Jane's red wool frock was a welcome change from her usual blue jeans. Victoria, with rather marked resignation, shut off the set but managed a polite smile. The menfolk (four, if Ronnie was included) calculated the distance to the hall doorway (although I may have imagined this) before they resumed possession of their chairs.

I must say, I could not complain of lack of attention as I set forth the framework of Miss Mary's idea. Her economic arguments appealed more to the masculine point of view, perhaps, but none of my hearers was in a position to be indifferent to shopping costs. Jane argued, but not very convincingly, that trying to save money on Christmas gifts indicated a parsimonious character—"stingy" was her word, I think—but Ronnie, whose finances were always low, told her, in brotherly fashion, not to be silly. Not, he admitted, that the question of Christmas gifts wasn't a problem. It was all very well for the women not to worry, he said, but they could sew and crochet and knit.

"And cook," Jane put in.

"It's the men who have it hard," Ronnie stated, his good-looking young face so dejected that I felt I must come to the rescue.

"You, and the other men"—why not stretch a point in the interest of diplomacy?—"have *time*," I suggested. "And that's not all. Grandpa Lane and Mr. Hubbard are both clever with tools, and Mr. Coleman has a car. There are dozens of gift suggestions you can all produce, if you really go to work on your lists."

"It's one of Miss Mary's better ideas, Melinda," Elizabeth Hubbard said to me later. "For years I've been wanting to try something like this, but I never got it worked out in my mind. The children in school make all their gifts—you'd think adults would learn something from their example."

"Elizabeth's always been a very contented woman," was

Grandma Lane's reaction when I reported the gist of this conversation. "She's never happened to want a lot of jewelry or a fur coat."

As might have been expected, the twins were the most enthusiastic supporters of the Christmas Plan, as Jane referred to it, her emphasis capitalizing the words. She had promptly decided to make baby-sitting her main "gift," and in less than a week she had a list to show me, with her friends all neatly "graded," she explained.

"I'll sit three times free for my best friends—and for relatives," she told me. "Once is enough for the others."

For those in the family circle she had an elaborate and, I must admit, practical set of plans. These ranged from reading aloud to Grandma Lane (whose idea of luxury it was to be able to knit and be entertained at the same time) to making her mother a present of three Saturdays on which she, Jane, would be available for anything her mother might require.

Ronnie, I learned, would content himself by running errands. He pointed out, with some justification, that everyone he knew regarded a teen-age boy as one designed for the sole purpose of running errands. He would also attempt to teach the children to skate.

I was curious to hear how Grandpa, Miles Hubbard, and Reade Coleman would decide their gift problems, and it was Victoria who told me. She herself had been placed in a quandary, she confided, since, unlike Grandma Lane and Elizabeth Hubbard, she could not knit or crochet and her cooking ability was limited to making instant coffee. After long deliberation, she said, she had finally decided to learn to play bridge. She hated cards, but if she made herself available as a partner she could provide the fourth so often needed not only in the house but also among her friends. I wondered a little what the three men, all good players, would think of this self-sacrifice, but then, Victoria might prove to be the best player of them all. It has happened.

And what, I asked tactfully, did she suppose the men planned to do in the way of gift giving? Or didn't she know?

Victoria knew—how could she help it, she demanded, when they talked of nothing else? There were times, she said, when the thought of living alone, in her own apartment, fulfilled her dreams of heaven.

"Grandpa Lane will promise to take Wednesday for a walk three times a day," she announced. "As it is now, the poor dog doesn't begin to get enough exercise. The twins are supposed to walk him, but they always have other things to do."

Miles Hubbard, she continued, would offer to attend to all small repairs, promptly. The accent, he meant to stress, would be on the promptness. He was handy with tools, too, but he could listen to a leaky faucet for a month without getting nervous. This statement I recognized as one made by his wife.

Reade Coleman, Victoria said, intended to put his car at the disposal of the family one day a week for a year. The only stipulation was that he must drive.

"It's really handsome of him," Victoria admitted. "The way he babies that car, I expect to see him take it crackers and milk almost any morning."

Jane, Victoria went on, had devised a way for the presentation of these unusual gifts. Miss Mary was sending a Christmas tree for the living room, and Jane was to collect a typewritten statement from each member of the family, setting forth his or her promised contribution. Victoria explained that she and Jane were to do the typing of these "scrolls," which were to be rolled, tied with red ribbon, and hung upon the tree. All in all, it was well thought out and, since I seemed to be the only one to have any misgivings, I thought it best to keep still.

The trouble was that no one, except me, appeared to remember that Miss Mary's experiment had been for one year and that one year was fast coming to an end. She was quite plainly bored with the *status quo* and eager to try something else. What the something else was she didn't know, and I had an uneasy feeling that she might expect me to offer suggestions. I was fairly certain that she would be willing for the present situation to continue, but then again she had not said so. And I was inclined to think that some of the experimental family would be glad to terminate the agreement. There was nothing definite on which to base my uneasiness, and until I had a lead it seemed wiser to say nothing.

It was Victoria May who asked me if I "knew anything" about the building project on the north side of Acton. This was an enormous plan, which was getting increasing attention not only in the city daily papers but throughout the state. According to the stories already published, a large syndicate was building three apartment houses, each covering a full block. These buildings would be connected by bridges above the first floor—each building was to be thirty stories high—and when they were completed, there would be one thousand apartments offered for rent.

Naturally, I had read the publicity fostered by this ambitious undertaking—it was manna to the Acton newspapers, always hard up for local excitement—and I had a feeling, but no proof, that some of Miss Mary's money was behind the syndicate. The whole thing had been a well-kept secret during the acquisition and demolition of the run-down and in some cases abandoned lodginghouses and shabby small shops, and it was not until the new apartments were going up that the syndicate had tactfully started to woo the press.

I was a little surprised by Victoria's question, but I agreed with her that it would be interesting to inspect the first apartments to be opened to the public the following week, and to look over the floor plans for the other two buildings. She had never lived in a new apartment, Victoria said wistfully. It must be pleasant to start off with all new fixtures, didn't I think?

Truthfully, I did think so, but Miss Mary kept me so busy the next week that I had no time to wonder if Victoria had inspected the new apartments and, if so, what she thought of them. Miss Mary planned to spend the winter in Florida, as usual, but made it clear that she intended to keep an eye on the family and its activities. Once she said something that made me wonder if she could be planning to duplicate the experiment, and even the shadow of the possibility made me shudder. Later, I learned that during the week I was absorbed in carrying out a new set of her endless directions the subject of the apartment houses became a fascinating interest to her experimental family. Ronnie and Jane, I believe, first listened skeptically to Victoria and then, once they had toured the project themselves, were wildly enthusiastic. They dragged their parents to the Nationale Royale (a name dreamed up by the syndicate, which also had insisted on the two es, the renting office'declared), and the kitchen equipment won the heart of Elizabeth Hubbard, while the garage arrangements fascinated Miles. The twins had set their hearts on having apartments of their own. They were to go to the state university in the fall, commuting from Acton. I knew that their parents had been saving for years to be able to send them to one of the larger colleges, but first Miles's father and then Elizabeth's mother had needed to be helped through long and painful and expensive illnesses. If each of the twins shared an apartment with three other students, their disappointment might be lessened. Besides, as Elizabeth said, learning to live away from home is a valuable lesson.

The passionate desire for secrecy was to puzzle me, when I had time to consider it. After having lived for almost a year in comparative friendliness and certainly some intimacy, why suddenly such marked withdrawals? It was so apparent that I could almost visualize the lines that separated the circle into distinct units. There had been no quarrels; indeed, when I visited the house after an absence of a little more than a week, there were no traces of friction. No one sought to back me into a corner to report on the "insufferable" behavior of anyone else—an occurrence I had come to expect—and not only was the general atmosphere peaceful, but it was mysteriously light-hearted as well.

But this I did not discover until after I had put Miss Mary and Minna, her devoted maid, on the Florida plane. Meanwhile I was dismayed to hear that Miss Mary intended to examine the possibility of setting up a second family circle—her own expression—in Florida. Somehow I did not feel that this first project had proved her theory: true, there had been no violent quarrels, but what an aunt of mine used to call "strained relations" had prevailed rather often. And I could not honestly assure Miss Mary that any affectionate ties had been developed, but then, perhaps I was in no position to judge.

It was the day after Miss Mary's departure, and I was returning a half-dozen library books she had forgotten to read, as well as to return, when I met Jane on the wide stone library steps.

"Hi!" She greeted me enthusiastically. "Why haven't you been to the house? You don't know what you're missing."

The alarm provoked by this statement was probably due to my age. What, I asked politely, had I been missing?

"Oh, things—" Jane's generation seldom supplies details. "Anyway, Uncle Reade was saying only last night that he thought perhaps Daddy had better send for you."

No, no one was ill, no, the Christmas preparations were going all right, yes, the plumber had fixed the furnace and the house was hot as—well, it was so hot day and night that no one except Grandpa and Grandma Lane could breathe.

"But Unkie says there are things you ought to know," Jane informed me cheerfully. "And Mother thinks it's time to have another round-table talk."

I promised to phone her mother that night. Jane's parting sentence, flung over her shoulder as she dashed down the steps, was scarcely reassuring.

"In a way, it's funny," she said.

Elizabeth Hubbard's unhurried, sincere voice *was* reassuring. She had intended to phone me and suggest a meeting, but had thought it wiser to wait until after Miss Mary had left for Florida.

"I—we—didn't want to upset her, you see," Elizabeth said.

No, there was nothing wrong, she added quickly. There was some surprising news, perhaps, but all of it was good, and there was not the slightest reason for me to feel uneasy.

She would make certain that everyone was at home the next evening but one, she promised, when I suggested that I come then. And she repeated that I was not to worry—nothing was wrong. Everything was just as usual.

There might be no cause for worry, I admitted to myself, when a few minutes after eight found us all seated around the beautifully polished table in the dining room. But if no worry, how to account for the tension? I looked around the table and saw that the knuckles of Grandma Lane's wrinkled hands, folded on the table before her, were white. But that might be because she had no knitting to relax her. Reade Coleman was beating a silent tattoo on one folded arm. Grandpa Lane scowled, a sure sign he was upset. Victoria May sat on the edge of her chair. She kept a forefinger on the muscle under her right eye, which twitched at intervals. As for the twins, they were so excited I would not have been surprised to see them burst into flames at any moment. Jane's lovely skin was flushed, and she tugged at a lock of her front hair. Ronnie fidgeted and kept clearing his throat. Only Miles and Elizabeth Hubbard looked or acted as usual, but when Grandpa Lane sneezed Elizabeth almost jumped out of her chair.

I thought I'd better make my speech quickly and so perhaps relieve the evident strain.

"Miss Mary has made me the bearer of her Christmas good wishes," I said formally, conscious of the battery of eyes focused upon me. "She has written individual notes thanking each one of you for your splendid co-operation. She feels that you have made her experiment a very real success, and she hopes that you are all willing to continue it for another year. Since she will not be here for Christmas she has left me these—er—tokens of her appreciation to distribute."

I placed the small stack of white envelopes on the table before me. Each, I knew, contained a substantial check. It was impossible to read the expressions on the faces turned to me, but at least I had carried out Miss Mary's instructions.

Reade Coleman was the first to break the rather unnerving silence.

"You'll have to tell her—tell Miss Mary—that I can't accept her gift. Say I'm grateful and appreciative and all that, but it's impossible. Under no circumstances. It's impossible," he repeated.

I had been more or less prepared for refusals by the men— Miss Mary had rejected the suggestion that she make out joint checks for the Lanes and the Hubbards—but in view of the explanations I would have to make I felt entitled to ask his reason.

Reade, generally so self-possessed, appeared oddly disconcerted. His face flushed and he glanced wildly around the circle.

"Well, if you must know—" He scowled at me. After all, I was the one who had trapped him. "I've rented one of the apartments at the Nationale Royale."

He glared impartially at us all, and I must say the reaction surprised me. I would have expected them to show some interest in his future plans, but very little was said, and I distributed Miss Mary's Christmas envelopes with the feeling that something was decidedly wrong. I overheard Victoria May tell Grandma Lane that she thought his—Reade's—action underhanded, but this was perhaps because he had not asked her advice. At least, that was Jane Hubbard's opinion.

It was a decided surprise to be informed by my secretary, shortly after Christmas, that Victoria had telephoned for a noon appointment. She arrived promptly, of course—my watch was one minute late, but not Victoria—and almost before she was seated in the chair beside my desk she handed a familiar-looking white envelope to me.

"I'm returning it," she said.

I knew the envelope contained Miss Mary's check. It had not been opened. Victoria, not ordinarily at a loss for words, was definitely uneasy.

"I realize I should not have kept it this long," she said apologetically. "But it required a little time for me to make up my mind."

She dropped a glove, retrieved it, and said that she had always been opposed to snap judgments.

Since I had no idea what she was trying to say I thought it best to keep still. Victoria had refused to take off her heavy winter coat—she could stay only a few moments, she had told me—and I wondered how she could endure the heat of the office.

"I think you're probably the only one who will know how I feel," she started off suddenly, with a rush of words. "A one-and-a-half-room unit and a restaurant on the first floor. I hate to cook."

There is a limit to everyone's patience, and mine had been reached.

"What on earth are you talking about?" I snapped. "What restaurant and where?"

Victoria withered me with a single glance. She had been trying to tell me, she said calmly, that she had inspected the efficiency apartments to be offered by the Nationale Royale.

"They're finishing sample apartments," she explained. "I brought away one of the floor plans. Mine is going to be on the fourteenth floor."

Yes, she had rented one of the efficiency apartments, she said, with an odd air of confession. It would be ready about the time her one-year "obligation," as she termed it, to Miss Mary had been met.

"Naturally I can't accept her Christmas gift," she continued. "But I'll write and thank her. The apartment I picked out has a lot of built-in furniture. Of course it will be simply wonderful to be alone."

This was positively the longest speech I had ever heard her make, and a loquacious Victoria was little less than astonishing.

"You have no idea," she was saying now, "how difficult it has been. In a measure I am to blame, of course, but at my age it is difficult to change one's nature."

The trouble with these strong, silent types, I reflected nervously, is that they are apt to release their pent-up emotions without warning.

"There have been times when I've told myself that I'd go mad if I had to spend one more evening in that living room, listening to the flood of inane chatter. Night after night—"

I was quite honestly appalled. I had had no idea she had felt like that, I said penitently.

It was all right now, Victoria assured me. As soon as she had signed the lease for the efficiency apartment she had felt relaxed.

"I don't mind waiting—the agent told me there are always delays." She stood up, buttoned her coat. "I don't think I'll be missed by the family circle," she added unexpectedly. "I was born a poor mixer."

The reams of publicity accorded the Nationale Royale were almost as spectacular as the project itself, and I found myself reading with fascinated attention detailed descriptions of the conveniences, the decorations, and the elaborate precautions for the safety and comfort of future tenants.

I had been to one of the small outlying farms (Miss Mary owned several, all rented profitably) one clear, cold afternoon, and was driving home, when ahead of me on Acton's busy main street I sighted Grandma Lane and the three children. Robert, Leila, and Holly were trying to scoop up enough snow from the gutter to make snowballs—with the exception of the Thanksgiving storm, we had had almost no snow—and Grandma was walking slowly, as if tired.

My offer of a lift was accepted enthusiastically, and after a brief argument about why children should take the back seat and an elderly lady sit beside the driver we were on our way. The children had wanted to see the "big new house" where, when it was finished, more than a thousand people would live, and Grandma had promised to take them there. But she had not realized the distance and had never, so she assured me, been more glad to be offered a lift.

"I'm all right, if it wasn't for my legs," she said valiantly. "Besides, it's a long walk, and I was wondering how I would ever get the children home, once we were ready to come back. Holly's legs give out, too, only she won't admit it."

Faced by four disappointed explorers, what could I do but offer to drive them to the Nationale Royale, even though, as I warned them, there would not be much to see. Two or three furnished apartments were open for inspection, but Robert had set his heart on "going to the top," however high that might be, and Leila was determined to see the indoor playrooms someone had mentioned in her hearing.

"I'm so glad you met us," Grandma Lane said, in a low voice, as we stopped for a traffic light. "I've been wanting to tell you something for a long time. But I never seem to get a minute to myself."

This complaint was beginning to have a familiar ring, and I'm afraid I looked at her rather suspiciously.

"It's about these new apartments," she continued jerkily, as the light changed. "Caspar and I have been looking at them."

She fumbled in her bag and brought out Miss Mary's Christmas envelopes.

"We don't feel it would be right to accept it," she said, still trying to keep her voice low. "We've signed up for one of the three-and-a-half-room apartments. They're going to be just lovely."

She and Caspar were both anxious to have me tell Miss Mary how grateful they were to her for having enabled them to save a substantial amount of money in the past year. Nothing would have induced them to utter a complaint while they were "beholden" to her for so much—indeed, if it had not been for her generosity they probably would not have been able to afford one of the new apartments.

"But, my dear, do you know, if I had to live through it again I think I should lose my mind!" Her voice trembled and the blue eyes behind her spectacles were tragic. "Everyone *talks* so much!"

We had reached the development, and the children were clamoring to get out. The renting agent opened the door of his snug little office and greeted us like old friends. At least, he recognized Grandma Lane. She and "the old gentleman" had come nearly every day to watch the progress of the building, he said.

The children, momentarily awed by the towering steel, brick, and stone structures, the mammoth cranes, the general noise and apparent confusion, were content to remain near the car. What we were seeing, the young and voluble agent told us, was virtually a town under construction. A complete shopping center was in the plans, a recreation center for adults, a playground for children. He prophesied that the apartments would be fully rented long before construction was finished. All apartments were to be soundproof.

"We emphasize privacy," he said, smiling at Grandma Lane. "That's what you wanted, isn't it?"

I don't know why I should have been surprised to have Jane Hubbard phone me a few days later and ask for an appointment. I might have known what the "something important" she was anxious to discuss with me was to be. She arrived only fifteen minutes late, looking very pretty in red slacks and sweater that set off her dark eyes and hair.

"I'm sure you'll understand," she began, as soon as she was seated. "In fact, you're almost the only one we can count on to understand and be reasonable."

"Don't use up all the butter at once," I advised her. "And who is 'we'?"

She had not expected me to be difficult, she retorted, her dark eyes reproachful. She and Ronnie both counted on my help.

"What do you want to do that your parents won't approve of?" I asked, rather brutally, and was informed that I was just like all the others.

"You don't even ask what I want to tell you," she complained.

This was true. I apologized and said I was ready to listen.

"Well, it's about the new apartments—the Nationale Royale development." Jane hurried into speech, but broke off abruptly. "What's the matter?" she demanded.

Nothing was the matter, I assured her.

"I thought you looked kind of funny. Well, anyway, Ronnie and I have been thinking about having apartments of our own. Next fall, when we're in college."

They had everything planned out, Jane said, still eying me in some alarm—I probably "looked funny" again. She and three other girls would share one apartment, and Ronnie another with three fellows.

"It wouldn't cost too much that way." Jane leaned forward, her pretty face serious. "Melinda," she whispered, "you have no idea how sick and tired I am of living with a lot of people."

She exempted her parents in the next breath, but was there any earthly reason why everyone else had to be in everyone else's pocket?

Cautiously I pointed out that four girls sharing an apartment couldn't expect to have much personal privacy. That, I of course was told, was perfectly silly.

"It's entirely different," Jane insisted. "But I thought perhaps you could say something to Mums? She isn't the type—at least I don't think she's the type—to get hysterical when she hears her children want to leave home, but you never can tell, can you? I thought someone like you—you have loads of tact—could break it to her gradually, kind of."

A round-table session would give her an opportunity to talk about an apartment—that was, if she didn't want to talk it over privately, I said. And was there any reason why Ronnie should not express his own desire to move into an apartment?

"Is he trying to hide behind your skirts—er—I mean slacks?"

Jane tried to look wounded and succeeded only in giggling. Ronnie, she said, was firmly convinced that his mother would burst into tears. He couldn't bear to see her cry.

"There's always the chance that she might shed tears of

joy," I suggested. "Anyway, if Ronnie is old enough to live away from home he's old enough to present his own case clearly. Tell him I said so."

I do not think that I am especially sensitive to atmosphere, but when we were all assembled around the highly polished dining-room table early the following week I was definitely conscious of what, for lack of a better word, I'd call tension. The children were in bed—I was reminded of a remark of Reade Coleman's to the effect that children should stay in bed until they were fourteen years old—and Ronnie kept glancing toward me: I think he expected me to signal him when to burst into speech.

But it was Elizabeth Hubbard who, to the general surprise, took the initiative. She looked composed and cheerful, not at all, I thought afterward, like a woman about to drop a bombshell.

"This is probably the best time to tell you all—" she patted her back hair, a gesture Jane had once told me is a nervous gesture of middle-aged women—"that we have signed a lease on a three-bedroom apartment in the Nationale Royale project."

If she had meant to surprise us, the attempt was a complete success. But it was Ronnie who was the first to recover his power of speech. He mumbled, "Oh, no!" as his father placed two of the now familiar white envelopes on the table.

"We're returning them with sincere thanks," Miles Hubbard said, smiling at me.

Elizabeth was staring at her twins perplexedly.

"Aren't you pleased?" she asked them. "The rooms are lovely."

Jane, seated across the table from Ronnie, waited for him to speak, but when he said nothing she shrugged her shoulders.

"It's only that Ronnie and I want to move out, Mums," she

said. "Have our own apartments, I mean. It won't cost too much, splitting the rent four ways."

"Where on earth would you live?" Elizabeth was as clearly bewildered as if she saw her children facing a desert. And Jane's matter-of-fact reply did nothing to lessen her anxiety.

"Why, in the Nationale Royale, of course," Jane said.

Poor Elizabeth could only repeat, "In the Nationale Royale? You mean you and Ronnie want your own apartments? When you could live at home?"

"You don't understand, Mums." Ronnie was kind if condescending. "You don't understand at all. What Jane and I want is some natural privacy. In this house, you can't sneeze without somebody handing you the aspirin bottle."

Elizabeth looked so stricken that even her children could see she had had a shock. Jane addressed herself to her father.

"If we were going to one of the big universities, we couldn't live at home. And I don't see why, just because we'll go to BB" (the state university) "this fall, we should be penalized. Sharing an apartment is economical. And, don't you see, we want to get out!"

Miles Hubbard's eyes met mine, and in that instant the great, fundamental weakness in Miss Mary's plan became painfully clear. I wondered if they all saw it. Miles and Elizabeth had never been able to save any substantial amount since their marriage more than twenty years ago. Those long and expensive illnesses of both their parents had been a constant drain, and there had been a sister of Elizabeth's institutionalized for years, but not before she had crippled a child with her car. The heavy damages awarded the little victim were still a drain on the Hubbards' income, but they had volunteered to assume the debt.

But surely their own children were to be considered, I had argued more than once with Elizabeth, who had the gentle obstinacy that is stronger than iron. The children, she always assured me, were not being deprived of any essentials, and how could the younger generation be better taught to assume, not evade, responsibility than by example?

"I think," Miles Hubbard was saying, in his deep voice that carried authority, "that we'll have to cancel that lease, Libby. You and I will take a smaller apartment and underwrite the kids for a year. We may all like that for a *new* experiment."

It was Grandma Lane who asked about the children. They could not, she said, in her matter-of-fact way, be expected to live alone in the house, and it was equally ridiculous to expect them to take an apartment on their own. I was glad to be able to announce that early in the new year—and probably long before the Nationale Royale was opened to tenants—the children's parents would have returned.

"I read where they've sold their big barn of a town house," Victoria said. "Wouldn't it be odd if they should take one of the new apartments? Some of them have six or seven rooms."

"Do you suppose Miss Mary will want to live there?" Victoria asked suddenly.

I had no idea, but this seemed to me to be a propitious moment to put a question that had been nagging me for some time.

"This family experiment of Miss Mary's—do you think it has proved anything?" I asked.

"No." Reade Coleman answered too quickly, and the others said nothing.

But Jane spoke slowly before the silence became too awkward.

"Ronnie and I've been talking about that." She tugged at a lock of hair and glanced appealingly around the table. "We think—I may not be saying it right, but we think it's because you can't, or shouldn't, use people to prove a theory. What I mean is, it's all right to experiment, but not with people."

I thought she had put it very well, and so did her audience, if the heads nodding in agreement meant anything.

"Well then, come the first of the year we'll no longer be together." Victoria sighed, her tone suddenly nostalgic, but her face expressed satisfaction.

And Jane grinned at her impishly.

"Don't forget, we can still be under one roof," she said.